Drunken NIGHTS

Bibi Norman

contents

CHAPTER 1

May 8, 2022

Dani

As I sway back and forth, my eyes are closed, enjoying the club's electric feeling tonight. With a beer in one hand and my best friend's waist in the other, life couldn't get any better.

Maria grabs my hand, beelining us to the bar. I trample over my own two feet as the 4 beers and 3 shots of vodka start to kick in. At this point, I don't think I can even walk straight... Maybe that's because I'm not.

Slamming into the bar's edge, I come to a halt as Maria falls over onto a bar stool laughing. I glare at her, groaning from the pain in my abdomen. "¡cabron!" (dumbass) I hiss at her.

"¡No seas gilipollas!" (Don't be an asshole) She laughs, rolling her eyes. "Gigi, two more shots!" she yells to the bartender. I don't think I have any more shots in me.

Maria and I finished the RN program at UC San Diego today and are now licensed RN's. We both received a job at Scripps Memorial hospital and will be starting Monday morning, so we're out celebrating hard before the party life gets taken from how much work we are about to endure.

Gigi slides us our shots, and Maria grabs hers lifting it for the 4 toast of the night. "To...." She can't think of another toast like a dumbass.

"Maria, just....shut it.... and take the....shot" I tried to get my words out, but they kept slipping. We both start laughing, and I raise my shot to hers, clinking the glasses before downing another.

The harsh liquid tickles the back of my throat as it goes down, my attention turns to someone behind my best friend. She's alone at the bar, playing on her phone. My eyes linger for a minute over her long dark straight hair and her nude plumed lips.

The strobe lights hit perfectly as her light honey orbs find mine. I raise my beer bottle to her, and she politely smiles as a response. I can't seem to tear my eyes away as the music begins to fade in the background.

Maria hits my shoulder and pulls me out of my daydream. "Ow! What was that for?"

"¡Mira! Dani, you're drooling over that woman, grow some cojones and talk to her."

"I have Cojonazos!" slurring over my words. She makes a disgusted face, and I know I succeeded in grossing her out. But she is right. I should go talk to her.

Walking past Maria, I stumble a little but catch myself on the stool next to her. "Somebody better call God because he's missing an angel."

She starts laughing at my joke while shyly playing with the pink umbrella in her cocktail. "That was clever" I smile at the heavenly sound of her voice hitting my ears.

"I'm Dani," I say, clumsily putting my hand out for her to shake.

"Natalia," she answers back.

"Natalia, mmm, what a sexy name." She laughs again, and I know I'm getting somewhere. "So, what brings you here alone tonight?"

"It's my birthday." My eyes grow big.

"Now, what is a beautiful woman like you doing alone on your birthday?"

She shrugs. "I came with my friend and her boyfriend but... they left me."

"Well, that's not very nice of them. If you were my friend, I'd stick with you all night long." emphasizing on the friend parts.

"Ha, that was smooth, but unless you have a little bit more in between your legs... I don't think this will work" I'm a little offended yet intrigued, knowing I have exactly what she wants between my legs.

"Mmm, well, you might just be surprised by what's down there," she raises an eyebrow at me, and I smirk at her curiosity.

The song in the club switches to reggaeton, and I take this as my opportunity to get her up. "Would you like to dance with me?" she looks at me as if she's thinking before shyly nodding a yes. I place my hand out for her to grab, pulling her onto the dance floor.

The music blares through the club speakers as she begins to sway against my hips. I try to control myself, but her body is that of a goddess. My hands find her hips brushing against the black leather.

As her ass rubs against my front, my member starts to grow from the contact. She stiffens and turns around to face me. She looks down at my jeans that have grown tighter around my arousal and back up to me.

She smirks, "If I wasn't as drunk as I was right now, I'd be questioning how this is possible, but It's my birthday... and I want to have a good time."

I raise an eyebrow at her "Ey Princesa, the best way to spend your birthday is in your birthday suit. ¿Falso?"

She wraps her arms around my neck, pulling my face closer to her. "Sí Tienes razón" (Yes, you're right) She whispers against my lips. I smile at her, knowing Spanish, as she leans further into me, brushing her soft lips against mine.

I stop swaying to the music and focus on the feeling of her smooth lips. It starts out soft and gradually intensifies as my fingers roam through her thick hair.

It's as if we are alone and there aren't hundreds of people dancing around us. Her slick tongue grazes against my bottom, and I tilt my head, giving her access.

Her moist tongue coats mine as they gracefully twirl in sync. I feel as her tongue flicks the back of my throat, and I deepen the kiss letting out an unexpected moan.

My fingers grip harder onto her locks as the fire grows from the pit of my stomach. I want more from her, but she pulls back, giggling from the kiss we just shared.

She grabs my hand and turns around, continuing to grind on my hips like the kiss never occurred. I shake the daze of what just happened out of my head and continue to dance along with her.

After 2 more beers and another shot, we are both hammered and sloppily grinding on one another. There was a point she took her phone out and recorded herself kissing me again. Her excuse was she wanted to remember some part of her birthday. Which I didn't mind.

An upbeat bachata mix comes on, and I grab her hand, spinning her out and back into me. We can stop laughing, and our eyes never leave each other.

She pulls me closer to her, sensually grinding her pelvis against my thigh as we move to the beat. I get heated, and she feels me grow against her again. "Take me somewhere," she whispers into my ears.

I smile, grabbing her hand, running out of the club, forgetting about Maria, and hailing a cab. When one comes near, I open the door for her, missing the handle at first, then successfully grabbing it the second time.

"It's not... funny!" I try to get out as she makes fun of my clumsiness. I watch as she eloquently gets into the car as if she hasn't had a single drink. I give the driver the address to the nearest hotel, and he nods, driving off.

She starts to suck on my neck, and I can see the cab driver's eyes linger in the rearview mirror. I grab her chin, moving her to where my lips are on her ear. "Let's give him a show."

She bites her plumed bottom lip, and I use my thumb to pull it out before connecting our mouths again. My finger trails up her thigh, making my way to her center. I can feel the heat radiating off of her core as I place my palm over the leather.

A moan leaves her throat, and we jump as the car swerves into the other lane then back straight. Natalia busts out laughing and shields her embarrassed face into my neck.

He drives into the hotel front, and I grab her hand leading her into the lobby. We waste no time getting a room then getting onto the elevator. Thankfully nobody is on with us, allowing me to corner her and steal another heated kiss.

The elevator dings, and the doors open as I'm pulled along to the room. I don't even have a chance to close the door before she pushes me into the bed, and I fall over in amusement.

"Eager are we, Princesa."

She doesn't say anything, just closes the door and locks it before prancing over to me. She starts to unbutton my jeans, and I sit upon my elbows to watch.

Her finger grazes across the zipper, and my eyes close as a slight moan leaves my throat. She grabs both my pants and boxers and pulls them down in one swift move leaving my dick standing straight up hard as can be. A loud gasp causes my eyes to shoot open, and I see her there with her hands over her mouth in shock.

"What the Fuc... You actually have a dick!?" Her eyes grow big, and words are slurred, and I can't help laughing at her response to my excited friend.

I'm used to this reaction being intersex... Many women don't know how to take it, but I'm too drunk to care about her response.

I keep laughing at her. "Why are you laughing?" She rolls her eyes.

"Because I told you earlier, you'd be surprised at what's down there."

She looks down at it, and I can tell she is still aroused by it. She bites her lip and starts to get shy again, "You can come back over here. It won't bite."

She crosses her arms and smacks her lips. My eyes travel down her full figure. Her curves dip in all the right places. "I know that! But damn, it's so big," she says back.

I smirk at her. "All 8 inches, baby, in the flesh" she smiles at me and shakes her head.

"You better be lucky I'm drunk and horny as shit." I take that as my cue to continue. I lift my shirt off, leaving me completely naked, and lurch back over to her.

I gently kiss down her cheek to her neckline and begin to suck on her pressure point. My hands travel to her shirt, pulling it above her head and sloppily grabbing her mouth with mine again.

My hands instantly find her large round breast and give them a squeeze. Her moans are music to my ears as I grab her ass, pulling her up letting her wrap her legs around my hips.

I toss her on the bed, and she giggles and starts to hurriedly unbutton her leather pants. She has a hard time getting them off, and I grab the bottom cuffs of both pants legs pulling with strength, causing me to fall on my ass and them to fall on the ground with me.

"Damn, girl... They are like glued to your ass."

She unhooks her bra and pulls her panties down, leaving herself just as exposed as I. "Shut up and get over here."

I drunkenly stumble back off the floor to the bed and kiss her. Our lips mesh together, and she bites my bottom lip pulling it with her.

I feel her warm palm around my shaft, setting me at her entrance with one hand and grabbing my hip with the other to push me into her. She lets out a moan as all of me slips into her wet core with no problem.

Her back arches as I slowly move out of her, thrusting hardback in. As I continue to stroke into her, I watch as her eyes roll back, enjoying my length. "You're so wet."

I feel the sharpness of her fingernails digging into my back as the sweat drips from our bodies. Penetrating her walls deeper and deeper as she comes closer to a mini orgasm.

Slowly moving in and out of her, I help her ride it out, then abruptly pull out, grabbing both of her hips and flipping her. I just as fast plunge back into the depths of her moist core, earning a scream from her. I grip her round ass as it jiggles in front of me. Admiring how plumped it is.

Slamming into her from behind as she dips her back lower, trying to get more. Running my fingers down her arched spine and leaned over to bite her cheek. Laying a hard smack against it as she presses back into me, helping me trace my own orgasm. I watch as she grips the sheets in front of her for support from the intensely intoxicated high we are having.

Beads of sweat continue to accumulate as drops fall from her face. Our breathing is increasing, as is our speed.

"Shit, you feel so good," I moan, thrusting harder into her. She starts to rock back into me, and I can feel my balls slapping against her clit.

"Yesss. Right there aaaaaa," She can't take it anymore, and I feel her walls tightly take hold of my member, keeping me in place as she screams in ecstasy. The sound of her pushes me over, and I burst inside of her filling her cores with my juices.

I fall over onto her back, and we both lay there soaked and sticky, connected to each other. I pull out of her, and she moans to the sensitivity. Breathing heavily, I roll over onto my back, trying to catch my breath and staring at the ceiling.

"Damn, that was amazing," I say, panting for air. Light snores are heard next to me from her side, and I lean over to see I put her to sleep. I lay back down and sighed, following right after her. This was one drunken night to remember.

CHAPTER 2

February 8, 2023

"How's the baby boy Lisa?" I say, walking into my patience room, grabbing her new bundle of joy from his hospital crib.

"He's a little fussy this morning. I think he's ready to eat," she says, smiling big at me and reaching her arms out for the baby.

"That he is. Let's see if we can get him to latch today" I give the mother her new baby, and she brings his mouth to her nipple. He jerks his head in the beginning but soon latches and begins to eat.

"There we go. He just needed a little help," I say, watching her smile and run her finger through the baby's curly hair. I take a look at her chart to see when she will be discharged and then walk out to make my rounds.

A smack lands on my ass as I jump and turn to see Maria. "¡Mierda! Maria, that hurt," I say, trying to rub the stink away.

"Aww, poor baby! Get over it," she stands beside me, reviewing her own charts. The phone rings, and the receptionist answers it.

Maria and I exchange glances, curious about the latest developments on the OB floor. After a series of affirmative and negative responses, she hangs up and begins typing on her computer.

"Anything interesting?"

"Yeah. We have a 24-year-old woman on her way; her water broke, and she slipped in it, then called 9-1-1. The ambulance reported no injuries, but she's alone without any family. We're preparing a room for her arrival."

Maria and I both nod, swiftly completing our rounds to ensure we can actively participate in this event. As newly licensed RNs, we're eager to gain experience in the birthing unit.

Once we're finished, Nurse Manager Johns passes by us. "You two, come with me." I pick up the new chart and follow her instructions, making my way to the hospital room where the expectant mother awaits.

Nurse Johns knocks on the door, and a faint voice responds, "Come in." We enter and find a woman lying on her side, clearly in pain.

She rolls over, and my heart instantly drops as well as the chart in my hands.

"Oh shit!"

The clipboard hits the floor, drawing everyone's attention. I quickly gather the scattered papers, only to meet the gaze of those familiar light brown eyes I first encountered nine months ago.

Maria leans over to me and whispers into my ears, "Is... Is that the woman you met at the club...?"

I swallow a lump in my throat and reluctantly nod. "Damn, looks like somebody might be a Papi," she whispers again, nudging me.

"Shut up, Maria," I reply lowly, ensuring our conversation remains unheard.

"Do you two know each other?" Dr. Johns asks, glancing between the pregnant woman and me.

"No!" "Yes," she said no, I said yes... damn, what have I gotten myself into?

"Alright. Nurse Gomez, will this create any issues here?" I clear my throat and shake my head no. "Good. Stay here and provide Natalia with the care she needs before active labor begins. Nurse Reyes, take over her charts and cover her rounds until Natalia here gives birth." We both nod, and Dr. Johns departs, with Maria following suit.

"You're lucky, Pendeja! Let me know how mi Sobrino turns out," Maria says, sticking her tongue out at me. I smack her with the clipboard, and she closes the door behind her, leaving just me and Natalia in the room.

I look over at Natalia, who lies on the bed, and my heart skips a beat. She appears even more radiant now. Her hair has grown longer, and her baby bump exudes a captivating aura. I mentally calculate the timing, wondering if this child could be mine.

"Can you stop looking at me like a piece of meat" I'm startled out of my daze and scratch the back of my neck, apologizing.

"Um... how are you?" I ask nervously, walking over to check her vital signs.

"Big and pregnant, as you can see." I nod, acknowledging her response, unsure of what else to say.

"Do you not have anyone here to sit with you while you give birth?" I ask, concerned. She shakes her head, indicating that she is alone. "Okay, well, if you'd like, I can stay with you and provide assistance during your contractions..."

"No," she cuts me off. "I don't need your helppp," a contraction hits, causing her to tense up, but takes it like a champ. I monitor the clock and observe the contraction on the monitor, noting its duration. As it subsides, she relaxes and resumes speaking, "I don't need you here. I'll be fine."

She sounds pissed at me, so I just nod, grabbing her chart. "Well, since you're still in early labor, and the contractions are spaced far apart at the moment... I'll leave you be. If they become more intense, please press the button, and I'll be right outside the door."

She ignores me, turning away to face the window. I exit her room, leaving the door slightly ajar, and settle at the nurse station across from her room. I can see her from here and think it's best to keep my distance.

"Loca! Did you ask her if that's your baby?" Maria says, slapping my back.

"No... she wants nothing to do with me" I sigh into the rolling chair.

"Damn, was the night that bad?"

"That's the thing... It was really good. I mean, from what I can remember. But when I woke up the next day, there was a note left on the nightstand that said, "Thanks for showing me a good time on my birthday," and she was gone."

Maria gives me a look of sympathy, and she quits with the jokes. "Well, maybe she'll come around and tell you if it's yours or not. Did you use protection that night?"

I shrug my shoulders. "We were so wasted I can't even remember, but my guess is no"

The nurse light goes off, and Maria gets up to check on one of her patients. 2 Hours go by. I watch from the nurse station, Natalia crying in pain and riding out each contraction.

I can't stand seeing her in pain and alone, so I walk over to her. "Natalia?"

She rolls over to look at me. "What do you want?" She asks, annoyed.

"I want to help. Your contractions are increasing in frequency. Would you like an epidural?"

"No, I'm fine." I can tell she's not but wanting to be tough about it. I just nod.

"Is there anything I can get you?" I say, walking over to her and rechecking her vital signs. She shakes her head no and rolls over again.

Taking this as my cue to give her some space, I return to the nurse station, maintaining a watchful eye from a distance. I opened her chart to read more about her since she doesn't want to open up to me. Why would she? We technically just met today regardless of a one-night stand. But she doesn't know me, and I don't know her.

Natalia Lopez. 24 years old. Birthday May 8th, the day we slept together. Hispanic. Both parents passed away 3 years ago. No siblings.

Address... I try not to learn it but with this photographic memory... it's already imprinted in my brain. I close her chart and start to spin in the chair, looking at the ceiling.

Four more hours pass, and Natalia reaches 9 cm dilation. Nurse Johns and I reenter the room, accompanied by a team of skilled healthcare professionals who gather around Natalia. The attending physician joins us, as we all form a supportive circle around Natalia as she prepares to begin pushing.

I can see the tears streaming down her face, and I know she's in a lot of pain. The obstetrician addresses Natalia directly, speaking in a gentle yet reassuring tone, "Okay, Natalia, it's almost time to push. Are you ready?"

She begins to cry and shakes her head no. "I can't! I can't!"

"Yes, you can, Natalia," The OB says while rolling her chair between her legs and getting into a position for her to push.

"No, I can't be a single mother. I don't know how to do this. This wasn't supposed to happen. I have nobody! I'm not ready." Her panic intensifies, and the machine beeps frantically in response to her escalating heart rate. She desperately gasps for air, her anxiety impeding her ability to take in deep, steady breaths. It is important for her to regain her composure to avoid further distress for both herself and the baby.

The attending obstetrician, recognizing the need for immediate intervention, exchanges a concerned glance around the room. Understanding the urgency, I step to her side and grab her hand. They are soft yet clammy from sweating. "Listen to me. You are not in this alone. You have me... and them," I say, pointing to the medical team in the room. "You can do this, Natalia."

She continues to shake her head no. I gently squeeze her hand and use my free hand to wipe away her tears. Leaning closer to her.

As nurses, it's normal to provide reassurance and encouragement to our patients when they feel scared during the pushing stage. However, I become very aware of the close proximity between me and this particular patient. In this moment, my hands offer comfort, one gently caressing the back of hers while the other tenderly grasps her chin, guiding her to meet my gaze. I can sense the unspoken curiosity in the room. My actions going beyond the typical boundaries of professional care. But I can't stop myself.

Feeling the weight of the unspoken tension, I close my eyes briefly, exhaling a deep sigh, and attempting to regain focus on the task at hand.

"Natalia, if this child is mine like I think it is... you are not alone in this. You will not be a single mother. I promise you." I meet her eyes, sensing a shift in her expression.

Her face softens, and a single tear falls from her eye. "Okay," she whispers, nodding slowly, her gaze still locked with mine.

"Alright! Let's prepare the room for the arrival of your baby. Natalia, when I instruct you to push, give it your all," The OB declares.

The room springs into action as everyone collaborates to make the necessary arrangements. The doctor positions herself to assist with the baby's delivery. "Okay, the baby is descending. Are you ready?"

Natalia looks at me for reassurance, and I squeeze her hand, letting her know it's okay. "Yes," she says, answering her back, but her eyes never leave mine.

She begins to push, and the room fills with the sound of her cries. I feel the pressure of her grip on my hand, but after an hour of determined effort, the wails of a newborn fill the air.

"It's a girl," the doctor announces, lifting the baby up for all to see. Natalia starts to cry while smiling at the baby. "Would you like to cut the umbilical cord?"

Natalia nods, and the attending obstetrician carefully turns the baby towards her, placing the scissors within her reach. She hesitates, the scissors poised above the cord. Her eyes shift to mine before handing the scissors to me instead. I pause for a second but ultimately take the scissors and cut the baby girl's cord in front of me. The OB gently places the vernix-covered newborn against Natalia's chest, and she holds her baby close, crying against her neck.

Sensing the need for privacy, I begin to step back, allowing them a room to bond. After ensuring Natalia's well-being, Nurse Manager Johns shifts her focus to the post-delivery responsibilities that lie ahead. Once these vital tasks are addressed, she turns her attention to me, "Can I see you outside really quick?"

Fuck I'm screwed. I follow her out of the room and into the hallway as she closes the door behind us.

"I heard what you told her in there."

CHAPTER 3

"I heard what you told her in there." I let my head fall, realizing that Nurse Manager Johns might take action and remove me from Natalia's case. Both Maria and I have worked hard to be under Nurse Manager Johns' supervision. "Thank you for not lying about knowing her. I noticed something and felt you needed to be in there. If you want, as we do the baby's first check-up, I can run the labs to find out if she's yours."

My head shoots up, surprised. "You can do that? You're not upset?"

"I can't be upset. You didn't know she was going to be the mother admitted here. If I had removed you from her case, you wouldn't have been able to support her during labor. And of course, we can run the test, Dani. I'm aware of you being intersex, nurses' gossip. And I understand the importance of knowing if the child is yours." I continue to fidget with my fingers, choosing to ignore the comment about nurses gossiping about me being intersex. After a brief moment, I finally nod in agreement, wanting to know the truth about the child's paternity.

"Okay, we'll run the test. You're relieved from my shift for the rest of the night." I look at her, confused. "Go in there and make sure she's okay. Giving birth is challenging, especially when one feels alone in this world."

She pats my back reassuringly before leaving me in the hallway. The other nurses exit Natalia's room, and I notice her inside, alone with her daughter on the bed. Despite my initial intention to enter, my feet feel paralyzed, refusing to move forward. A surge of anxiety courses through me, causing my chest to tighten and my heart to race. Overwhelmed by nerves, I can't seem to bring myself to go in there.

In an attempt to regain composure, I wipe my sweaty palms against my scrubs and turn away, seeking solace in an on-call overnight room. Closing the door behind me, I sink onto the bed, allowing my head to fall into my hands. Thoughts swirl in my mind, questioning how I ended up in this situation and how could I let this happen.

The door swings open, and it's Maria.

"Soooo.. are you a Papi?" She says, swaying her hips in a dance towards me.

"Stop saying that, Maria. I'm not a man. I might have a dick, but I have breasts, and I am a woman. So, if that child is mine... then yes... I'm a mother." She sighs and sits on the bed next to me. I know she means well, and her antics are to cheer me up. But this is all too much too fast.

"I'm sorry. I'll be more serious. I saw you and Nurse Johns talking. What did she say?"

"She would run the test to see if she is mine."

"And if she is...?"

I gave her a look, "¡Estúpida! Seriously. I'm going to take responsibility."

She laughs at me, "I'm kidding, Dani. Go talk to her then." I take her advice and get up to leave, but not before she slaps my ass again.

"Will you quit it puta?" I walk out the door and down the hall back to her room. The entry is slightly ajar with the lights off, and I see that she is sleeping with the baby in the hospital crib next to her bed.

I gain the courage and walk into the room, staying quiet to not wake them. I reach the crib, and the light from the bathroom is bright enough that I can see the baby's face.

Her head is full of dark straight hair, and she has the cutest pouty lips. Her face bears a striking resemblance to my own features, and a heavy sigh escapes my lips, realizing that there is a strong possibility she is my daughter. As the weight of this realization settles upon me, tears begin to well up in my eyes.

"Hi" I'm startled by that angelic voice, and I hurry to wipe the tear away, so she doesn't see.

"How are you feeling?" I ask her. She doesn't try to get up, only lying there on her side with her head resting on her arm.

"Better now that she's out," she says, smiling at the baby girl.

I nod at her, not knowing what else to say next. "Thank you for earlier... what you said to get me to push."

My eyes travel from the baby to her. "Is she mine, Natalia?" I ask bluntly.

Her face hardens, and she goes cold to me again. "No."

I look at her in disbelief, "Seriously?"

"She's not," she counters.

"So why does she have my hair?"

"She doesn't," she says, getting up looking at the sleeping baby.

"She has the same nose as me."

"So"

"Her lips are the same shape as mine."

"So!"

"Just admit she's mine, Natalia!"

"NO!"

"Why not!" I yell back.

"Because she's not!"

"You are lying," I'm starting to get frustrated. "Why won't you just say it?"

She breaks down, crying, pulling her knees to her chest. "Because it doesn't make sense."

"What doesn't?"

"You... This... Her." She says, pointing to her daughter. "We were so drunk... I wasn't thinking straight. I just thought I was imagining things when I noticed you had a penis. But when I woke up sober... There you were, naked. And we didn't use a condom. I was scared! I didn't understand how a woman could have a dick."

"You didn't just think I was a transsexual still in transition? Waiting for my boobs to be cut off?" I say, mocking her.

"I mean, I did at first... but then 4 weeks later, the symptoms were there, and I knew it wasn't my imagination. I didn't sleep with anyone else besides you. I didn't understand how it happened."

I smiled at her walking over and wiping her tears before sitting down on the bed next to her. "Well, let me clear things up then. My name is Danielle Gomez, but everyone calls me Dani. I'm 24 years old, and I was born intersex."

"Intersex?" I nod my head.

"Yup. I was born with both genitals with mainly woman features. At the age of puberty, I began to grow breasts. They aren't huge," I say, teasing. "But my parents chose my gender for me at birth. Where I underwent surgery to remove the ovarian tissue and close the vaginal slit as a newborn. When my breasts started coming in, I decided not to get surgery to remove them and keep both penis and breast. I wanted to feel unique." I smile.

"I go by female because it's the gender I most resonate with... soo if she is my child... then that makes me a mother." She lets her head fall, but I grab her chin, pulling her eyes back up to mine.

"I'm going to ask you again, Natalia," I say calmly to her. "Is she, my daughter?"

She nods her head with my fingers still attached to her chin. "Yes, she's yours" I smile and pull her into a hug. I don't know what possessed me to hug her, but it felt like the right thing to do while she was crying, and I was scared yet excited to be a mother. "I'm sorry I never found you to tell you. I... didn't know where to start looking. All I had was that stupid video of us making out at the club."

"It's okay. I'm not upset... So, I'm a mother," I say excitedly.

"Yes, Dani." she rolls her eyes, laughing at me. The baby starts to fuss herself awake, and Natalia reaches to grab her out of the crib.

"Hi, baby girl. Do you want to meet your other mommy?" She speaks softly to the infant and reaches to hand her to me. I swaddle the baby close to my chest as I hold onto my daughter for the first time.

She opens her eyes, and they are as light as Natalia's. I place my finger into her tiny palm, and she grabs hold of it. A smile forms, and I look at the beautiful woman next to me. "What's her name?"

"I was thinking Remona, Remi for short," she says, taking the baby's other hand.

I bring the baby up to my face and kiss her button nose. "Welcome to the world, baby Remona."

***

Natalia

"1.2..3..4" Since we woke up, I've been counting each toe and finger, still attempting to get past the surrealness of her actually being here. "You have all 10, baby girl," I whisper to my sleepy daughter.

I watch in amazement as her light brown eyes flutter shut while she is feeding off my breast. Running my fingers through her straight dark hair, a whiff of newborn smell fills my nose.

A light knock is heard at the door, and I give a low come in. Dani enters the room, closing the door behind her. My eyes travel over her body. Her hair is in a tight bun on top of her head. She's wearing a plain grey shirt tucked into tattered light blue jeans rolled at the bottom.

This androgynous style she has is slightly appealing to me, and damn, her jawline is sexy as hell. Ugh, it's so weird to think about a woman this way. I've always identified as straight and never considered the possibility of being interested in same sex before. It's new, and I find myself questioning everything I've known.

"Hey, Mamas," she says with a bright, toothy smile. I give a shy smile back and hurry to cover my breast from her view. "It's not like I haven't seen them before, Princesa."

I roll my eyes at her, still covering them. She sits in the seat across the room, and the feeling of her being so far gets to me. I pat the bed for her to come to sit, and she raises an eyebrow.

"Siéntate," I say under my breath, and she obliges. She walks over to the bed and sits down. My arms reach out with the sleeping baby, and she takes her gently into her own, not wanting to wake her.

"Good morning, Remonita," she whispers and lifts her to kiss her button nose. Her adding 'ita' to the end of Remona's name as a term of endearment towards our daughter makes my heart skip a beat. For the last 9 months, all I was worried about was doing this alone, and now that I found her, I might not have to.

The room goes quiet, and I watch as she sits in silence, admiring each part of Remi's features while she sleeps. It's as if she doesn't want to take her eyes off of her... like she isn't real.

"I feel the same way." Her eyes finally leave Remi to look at me, questioning what I mean. "She doesn't seem real... I keep counting her toes and fingers like she isn't real. Like I'll just wake up... and it'll all be a dream. Her...you."

"I can assure you I'm real" Remona starts to get a little fussy. She gives me a smirk that fills my belly with butterflies. "Shhhhh," she whispers and rocks her back to sleep, "And she... is definitely real. She's not going anywhere, Natalia. New mothers sometimes get this feeling. It's different carrying them and truly holding them in the flesh."

She lifts off the bed, pacing and rocking Remona. "You made a beautiful baby girl," she says, looking down at the bundle in her arms.

"We did," I say back.

She smiles, "Yeah, we did. Didn't we?"

The door opens, and a nurse walks in "oooo is this mi sobrina?" She squeals, running towards Dani. I'm guessing this is the lady that was with her at the club that night, from what I can remember.

Dani shakes her head and shushes her friend. "I'm sorry. Natalia, this is my best friend, Maria. Maria, this is Natalia."

She runs over to me and reaches to hug me. I'm a little startled, but I like the way she is welcoming. "It's nice to meet you."

"Same. Damn Danielle. ¡Ella es Hermosa!" (She is beautiful) She says back to Dani. She facepalms herself and shakes her head again at her friend. "What?" Maria asks.

"Muchas Gracias," I say, giggling back.

"Ay ¡perfecto! She is hot and knows Spanish. Shit, we live in Cali. They got tons of Ponchos out here, no offense."

"None taken." Maria walks back over to Dani to look at Remona, and I start to feel sleepy again. I know I have a couple more hours until they release the baby and me. We are just waiting on a few more results to ensure she has a good bill of health.

I hear them talking, but I slowly start to drift away. The amount of trust I put in this woman is odd because even though we barely know each other, I met her almost a year ago, and she doesn't feel like a stranger to my daughter or me, in any sort of way.

I think they notice how drowsy I am, and I hear Maria walk out of the room, shutting off the lights before closing the door. Dani takes a seat right in front of me, with our daughter still sleeping in her arms.

"Why don't you get some rest. I'll be right here."

"You don't have to be Dani. You can put her back in the crib and leave if you want," I yawn, getting up to put the baby back.

She is hesitant about giving her up, "Do you want me to leave?" she asks, and I can hear a hint of worry in her voice.

I sigh leaving the baby with her and laying back down. I turn away from her, not answering. I don't know if I want her to stay or leave. I don't know her at all. She might be Remona's mother... but I'm not gay... I don't like women. So, I want to keep this strictly about Remona.

I hear her behind me get up and place the baby in the crib. "I guess that's a yes," she says, a little pissed, storming out of the room before I can even say anything. She doesn't slam the door or even makes any loud sounds, but it's as if she did because the moment she leaves, Remi starts wailing.

I sit up to pick the fussing child up, coddling her close to my chest. I shush her while rocking her the way Dani did. "That wasn't very nice of me to do, was it?"

I lay back into the head of the bed, still rocking her. "Remi, what should I do?" I ask as if she will give me all the answers. I look down at her in my arms. "You look so much like her."

I sigh and raise my head back onto the pillow in the hopes that I can get a little bit more shut eye before I leave.

CHAPTER 4

February 10, 2023

It's clear that they had this planned, as Nurse Maria stands there with a smile on her face.

"I didn't need a ride, Dani." I insist, but she shakes her head.

"You were transported by ambulance. It's the least I can do to assist you two in getting back home."

I nod, trying to hide the slight smile on my face from the flowers she's holding. I was disrespectful to her earlier, and I don't deserve her to give me a ride home. She leans over to take Remona from my grasp, and I notice the car seat in the back. I'd like to say that I've prepared myself for having a child and have everything ready and set up in my home for a newborn baby. But I don't. I worked for most of my pregnancy and tried to forget I was pregnant. Not because I didn't want to be... but because I was afraid of actually becoming a mother and doing it alone.

She buckles Remona in the car seat and turns around to me. "Ready, Mamas." I lower my head, trying to hide my blush as she calls me that. "Hold this puta." She says to her friend, handing her the flowers. Maria rolls her eyes and I chuckle.

Dani gently supports me in transferring from the wheelchair to the passenger seat. She helps me in fastening my seatbelt and closing the door. I take a deep breath in as I turn to find our daughter fast asleep in the backseat. I reached back and took her little hand in mine. I flinch when the driver's side door opens, and Dani enters the car with the flowers. For a little while, I forgot she was still present. Remi's adorable face causes me to zone out at times, causing me to forget about the world around me.

"For you, Princesa."

"Thank you," I say almost in a whisper, taking the bouquet and smelling them.

"Of course. You can put your address on my phone." She handed me her phone, but it was locked. There is a picture of her best friend and her on the locked screen. It looks like the same outfit she was wearing the night we hooked up. I only remember because I have that video of us. They look drunk but happy. She has the biggest smile on her face. I turn the phone to her, showing the lock screen. "Oh, sorry, it's 0415. My birthday."

She says, turning the car on and waiting for me to put the address in. It's weird to have her phone in my hand and her password. I just met her, and it's like she has nothing to hide. Not that I'm looking for anything. This is strictly for the baby and allowing Dani to see her child. I kept the secret not on purpose from her but because I didn't know how to find her.

This isn't even my original hospital, so it feels like a lucky coincidence that I wound up in the hospital where the woman I slept with 9 months ago who got me pregnant worked. It's more than chance, and I'm grateful I'm not doing this alone. Although I'm not sure how well she'll do as a second mom. I barely know her, and the thought returns to haunt me. All the nice things I was feeling previously are now being trumped by worry.

I hand her back her phone with my address, and she drives out of the hospital parking lot in that direction. She turns the music on softly, and it's a song by Prince Royce. I watch from the side as she lightly sings and taps on the steering wheel, waiting at a red light. I turn to look out the window as we sit in silence with nothing but the music. I keep an eye on the trees as they go past us until we reach my house. She pulls into the lot and leans forward to read the sign.

"Um, am I at the right place? This says "G & N's Dance Studio""

"No, it's right. I live above the dance studio." I say, pointing to the second floor of my building.

"Oh. Okay, great." I unbuckle my seatbelt, and she comes rushing to my side of the car.

"I got it, Dani. I'm fine." I pull my arm from her grasp and stand up on my own.

'Oh... okay. I'll just get Remona." She walks back to her side of the car and grabs the car seat she brought. It's a nice one. One of those ones that convert from newborn all the way to like 5 years old. I hold the flowers in my hand as she follows me to the front of the building. I unlocked the studio and then locked it once we were both inside.

"My place is this way."

I point to the stairs and walk there. It's still painful after giving birth, and as I begin to walk the stairs, I know she can see the pain I'm in.

"Just take your time." She says behind me. I feel her hand against my back, guiding me up each step as she holds the car seat in her other hand.

"I got it," I grumbled, grabbing the handrail next to me taking on the remaining 6 steps. She retreats her hand, and I hear her whisper 'lo siento' under her breath.

We go to the top of the steps, and I unlock my front door. My place is currently a shambles as a result of all the baby stuff I had delivered here. The delivery men were kind enough to help me carry everything up the stairs.

The structure is old. It had previously been my mother's studio before being given to me. The second floor is a private residence, while the first floor is a dancing studio where she taught for 20 years. She let me have the place above the studio when I went off to college, so I didn't have to pay for college dorms.

Dani looks around, and I hold my back in pain. "You can just place her on the couch."

"Okay." She says, putting the car seat with the baby on the couch cushion. "Do...do you need help around the house. I don't mind if it means you get a little rest."

I gaze at her genuine eyes, then at my wreckage of a home. I nod slightly, and she moves over to assist me in getting onto the couch. I sit down and raise my feet to lie down completely. I don't even think about it twice before closing my eyes. I needed a moment to gather my thoughts.

My daughter's crying jolts me out of my slumber. I had no idea I had fallen asleep. Still, when I open my eyes, I see Dani pacing around the living room with Remona swaddled in a blanket.

She does that thing where she bounces her, and she starts to relax. Everything in my house has been cleaned, as far as I can tell. The clothes have been collected off the floor. Mine and the babies. I had done laundry for all of her new outfits but had never put them away. None were in sight. From where I am, the kitchen appears to have been thoroughly cleaned. The flowers she had brought me were now in a vase of water on the counter. Some of Remona's newborn items have been put together. Her playmat sat on the floor, along with a few baby toys, and the bouncer was pushed to the side. I never got around to any of this.

"How long was I asleep for?" My raspy voice breaks through the silence. She glances over her shoulder then entirely turns around. She looks at the clock.

"About 3 hours." I never got any of this done, and in 3 hours, she assembled a bunch of baby toys and cleaned my whole house.

"I think she's ready to feed again. She just woke up and is getting a little fussy."

I nod, and she brings Remi over to me. I take her and lift my shirt to allow the baby to attach. She walks behind the couch, and I notice she started assembling the crib. It's not completed yet, but it's about near done.

"Are you sure I was only asleep for 3 hours?"

"Mhmm," she hums, continuing to put pieces together.

"Thank you for cleaning up."

"Gracias por dar a luz a mi hija" (Thank you for giving birth to my daughter)

I chuckle. I sometimes assume she forgets or doesn't notice I speak Spanish like she did the first night we met. My father is Caucasian, and my mother was born and lived in Spain until she moved to the United States.

I strap Remona into the bouncer and set it to the setting that sways her in a figure eight. "Do you mind if I go take a quick shower?"

"Nope, I'll be here watching her and getting this set up for you."

I enter my room but stand off to the side so she can't see me, but I can see her. As she screwed in a piece, her muscles bulged. I groan to myself as I walk to the bathroom to take a shower. I'm putting a lot of faith in someone I've never met. But she is the mother of my child. There is no doubt about that. Since then, I haven't slept with anyone. I've been too preoccupied with work and making sure the bills are paid to keep this place running.

I stood in the water, remembering the night 9 months before. Because of the drunkenness, parts, and pieces are jumbled, but I recall some of it. Like the extra part in her pants. Her long hair and her razor-sharp jawline. I don't recall us having any sex. I was too slammed at that point, and so was she. It was as if the longer the night went on, the more messed up I became.

I get dressed after taking a shower and notice it's around 3 p.m. Tomorrow is a workday for me. I know I just had a baby, but I can't help myself. I'm on my own here, and I need to keep this place open for Mama. My door opens just as I'm going to slip my shirt over my head.

"Oh, I'm sorry. I thought you were still in the shower. I was just going to put this in here for you." I stand there, expressionless, staring at her as I pull my top all the way down. "I...is this where you want it?" She asks, stumbling over her words.

I nod and move to the door, keeping it wide for her as she drags the crib into my room. As I walk out of the room, I notice that my daughter is still sleeping. Damn, how much do these tiny creatures sleep for? It's as if she never wants to wake up until she needs a diaper change or a titty. I reach into the cabinet for a cup and pour myself some water. I'm startled by her being next to me, and I clutch my chest, trying to catch my breath.

"I'm sorry. I just... I got everything put together for you. I noticed all the baby clothes and hung them where you had the other clothes in the closet. I changed her twice already."

"Thank you," I say this while dropping my head and watching the ice cubes in my cup float around. I'm at a loss for words with her. This is all new to me.

"I don't want this to be Awkward, Natalia."

"It won't be. You're here for your daughter, I get that. Thank you for taking responsibility. Most men would claim it's not their child and leave it at that."

"It's a good thing I'm not a man, right?" She laughs, and I shrug my shoulders.

"Well, I actually live down the street. I left my number on the fridge if you need me. I just wanted to make sure you got to settle in okay."

She's leaving? Wait, how am I supposed to do this mothering thing? I don't know how to do any of this.

I mentally panicked but hid it perfectly from her as she walked away to say goodbye to her daughter.

I'm standing there with my eyes wide open, having a mild panic attack. One of those ones where the person appears to be alright on the surface but is experiencing intense anxiety and physical sensations of concern on the inside. An increase in heart rate, trembling of the hands. I look down at the cup in my hand, which is vigorously shaking. Turning around, I set the cup on the counter. Taking a few deep breaths.

"Okay, Remonita, you're all set. I'm going home for the night. Your Mommy is going to be amazing. I prepared everything for her so that you two could be as comfortable as possible. If you and Mommy need me, I'm just down the road. But I'm sure she won't. I'm confident she'll be an excellent mommy."

As I hear Dani kissing Remona over and over again, her tiny self becomes a little more vocal with cooing. My breathing slows, and the episode fades away with the sound of her words.

"Okay, I'm heading out. You have my number. Text or call whenever, and I'll be there. I'll be back in the morning to check in on your two, though. I took off for a few days just in case you need me."

"Okay," I reply in hushed tones, silently wishing she wouldn't leave.

She walks out the door, and I'm left alone. Until the baby starts crying again, like if she slammed the door and scared her. Which did not happen... again.

CHAPTER 5

February 11, 2023

"Okay little ones. Let's start your feet in the first position as we've practiced."

This is a beginner's class for toddlers. So, it's filled with the ages of 3-5. Class begins as I watch the little toddlers stand in front of me in their leotards and leggings. Some of their outfits are pinks and bright with sparkles, while others are plain black. There are a few boys in the class, which I love because we take pleasure in diversity here.

"Okay, we're going to take two Demi-pliés. That's right. Bend and stretch. A little lower, Tiffany. And again."

I walk around the room with Remona strapped on my chest, watching the kids do their exercises to start off class. This is what I do for work. I am a dance instructor. I teach all age groups and took over the company after my mother passed. I've been learning ballet at this studio since I was young as the children in front of me. I do ballet in my sleep now.

"Move your right arm to first position. There you go and open it in the second position. Go ahead and do your other arm."

Remi gets fussy on my chest, and I bounce her and rub her foot to get her to calm down. The children get giddy just hearing the newborn baby. They haven't got to meet her yet, but they were all here while I was pregnant.

"Demi-plié and stretch. Demi-plié and stretch." I walk around the room, instructing them and fixing the position of some of their tiny arms. As I pass by each, they raise their chins slightly to get a glimpse of the baby. I smile at how intrigued they are with her rather than their lessons.

"Look at your right fingertip and bring it in. Then look to your left and bring it down."

I let them hold the position until I reach the front of the dance room again. There is a giant mirror in front of them where they each can watch their stance to make sure it is correct. I grab the remote and press for the music to come on, and they go over their stretches again, this time with little instruction.

Class continues on, and for the most part, Remi stays quiet on my chest. I am tired and in pain, but I won't show that in front of the children and their parents. It's mostly dance moms here, and they can be quite intimidating. They are very judgy and think their children are the best over the others. They claim to be friends with each other, but when one child gets a solo over the other for competition days, it's all hell let loose between them.

I get a few dads in here supporting their daughters. Never really their sons. Most men don't take pride in their sons taking on ballet. Males are needed in dance. They could gain a lot of strength, flexibility, and confidence. It takes a lot for a male to overcome their confidence and get on stage in a mostly female dominating sport. Just as it would be for a female in a male sport. Plus, sometimes we need males for the lifting of the females in the dances. I think dads should take more pride in their sons joining just as their daughters.

The class soon comes to an end, and all the little kids crowd me to see the baby. It's still early morning, and Dani hasn't arrived yet. I know she wouldn't be happy seeing me on my feet. But I didn't know when Remi would come, and I didn't shut my classes down to spend some alone time with her. Plus, the parents would bite my head off if I randomly shut down classes. Their class fees pay my bills, and I don't need any lapse in payment.

I take a well-needed seat on the bench in the studio, and the kids waste no time coming my way. I hear tons of 'ooo's and 'awww's' as they get to finally see her. I take her out of the carrier on my chest and hold her insight for them.

"Okay, no touching the baby. Just look with your eyes." Wendy, one of the mothers, says, and I give her a faint smile to say thank you. She is one of the nicer ones, and her daughter is always quiet. She is newly divorced and keeps to herself for the most part.

"She has such a cute little nose." The oldest child says, and the other kids nod their heads vigorously. I hear the chime from the bell hooked to the front door of the studio. I look in the huge mirror to see Dani walking in with a box of donuts. I glance at the mothers, and a few of them are throwing googly eyes at her. A pinch of envy feels me and the green eyed monster seeps through. But I don't say anything; instead, I lower my head, looking back down at my daughter. Dani isn't mine, so I can't get jealous of other parents eyeing her.

"Donuts!" One of the toddlers' screams, and they all run away to Dani.

I can tell she is surprised by the number of creatures running her way and their grabby hands flying up towards her. She was hesitant at first, but I nod. I'm not sure the donuts were for them. But I don't want any, and these goblins will beg until they get some. So, if Dani is comfortable, she can give them to the kids.

"It's okay, mine can have one," Wendy says first. And Dani lowers the box for Tiffany to grab a donut. Soon other mothers are giving permission for their children and taking one for themself. Soon the box only has 2 left, and everyone is greedily eating.

"Hi, I'm Harper." A mother says, extending her hand. The other moms introduce themselves.

"I'm Dani." She finally says back as one mother's hand lingers too long in the palm of Dani's.

"Does your daughter dance here as well?" I want to speak up, but Dani answers before I can say anything.

"Actually. My daughter isn't old enough yet. But I'm sure once she is, her mother will put her in classes." She looks towards me and flashes that smirk that causes my heart to skip a beat. All the mothers turn my way. "If you ladies don't mind. Excuse me." She says, pushing through them to meet me.

"It's okay. You can stay seated." She says, lifting Remona out of my arms and rocking her. I can feel the daggers of a few of the mothers my way but decide to ignore them. Dani turns her back to them, stepping in front of me, cutting off my vision of them.

"Natalia, why are you out of the house?" Her tone shows a hint of annoyance, but it's only low enough for me to hear. I'm grateful because I don't need to be scolded in front of my class.

"I had work, Dani. I'm fine. I just have two classes today."

"You gave birth three days ago." She looks down at me, finally taking her eyes off our daughter.

"I'm fine." I reiterate.

"She is less than a week old. She shouldn't be around this many people."

"Nobody touched her. She is fine."

"That's not the point." She sighs. "Can I take her upstairs until you are done?" I nod my head and watch her take Remi up to my place.

The mothers watch her with lust in their eyes as Dani ascends the stairs out of their view. I clear my throat, and they all turn fast away from her direction.

"Tif and I are going to head out now. We'll see you Wednesday, Ms. Nat." Wendy says, leading her daughter out of the studio. The rest of the mothers bear their farewells and do the same thing. I wave bye to the little ones, and when the door shuts with the last people, I let out a deep breath and lower my head in my lap.

I groan to the pain I'm in. The door chimes, and I look up, not expecting anyone yet. My next class isn't for another 15 minutes. But I am met by my annoying best friend, Bailey. I stand up, and she gasps.

"Bitch... where is your stomach?" She questions in all shock. She left for the weekend with her boyfriend for their anniversary, and I hadn't had time to message her and tell her I had the baby.

"I... surprise," I say with a fake smile.

"Don't surprise me. What the hell happened, Natalia? She wasn't due for another week."

"Well, she had other plans. She was ready." She shakes her head and hugs me tightly.

"I was supposed to be there, jackass."

"I know it all happened so fast. I slipped down the stairs, and the next thing I knew, I was rushed to the hospital, and she came a few hours later. "

"A few hours. That was enough time to get on the phone and say, 'Hey, Bae, Remona is coming, so get your ass back here.'" Bae is the nickname I call her, short for Bailey. She lets go of me and looks down at my body. "When did you have her? I was gone for 4 days."

"Three days ago." Her eyes grow big.

"And you are up taking classes. What the hell is wrong with you? You definitely should have called me. I would have instructed your classes for you today."

"It was your anniversary. I didn't want to bother you, Bae."

"Bother me? Bitch I am your bestest friend. Jeff's little dick could have waited." We both start laughing, and she hugs me tight again. "I can't believe you're a mother now."

"Neither can I," I whisper against her shoulder. She pushes me back as if a switch goes off in her head. She searches around the studio, I guess looking for my daughter.

"Where is she?"

"Upstairs."

"By herself? Girl, do I need to call CPS." I chuckle.

"No... She's with her... other mother."

She furrows her brows.

"Other mother? Nat, what the fuck happened? I left for 4 days, and you have a baby and a new girlfriend you are calling your daughter's other mother. Shit, I need a drink." Same, but that's what got me here in the first place.

"No... it's... the women I told you about."

That crease in her face still hasn't left, and I poke it worrying about her getting wrinkles.

"The woman 9 months ago with the... penis. The one that knocked you up?" I nod my head. "Oh... Shit, I gotta see this."

She rushes up the stairs, and I tread behind her, holding onto the rail, trying to go as fast as her before she says something crazy.

She bursts in the door and stands there staring at what I presume to be Dani.

"Hi, there" Bailey giggles a little like a manic and pushes a strand behind her ear, waving her fingers at the woman in my living room. She panics and turns to me, waving her hands for me to hurry.

"Bitch I just had a baby. Give me a second."

"Shut the fuck up. Your ass is out here doing classes."

"Stairs aren't that easy." I roll my eyes but finally make it up to them. I walk past her and into my house, ignoring her and walking to my kitchen to grab water.

"Dani, this is my best friend, Bailey. Bailey, this is Remona's mother, Dani."

"Nice to meet you," Dani says as she lifts our daughter and whispers things to her. I can't hear her, but I know it's probably something sweet like she said yesterday before she left.

"You too... sooo you're the one that knocked my friend up?"

"Bae." I half-whisper half shout. Here she goes.

"And I presume you're the friend that left her on her birthday the night she got knocked up."

Bae looks back at me, shocked at Dani's response, and I shrug. "I like her," she mouths, scrunching her nose.

"So you have a penis?" I roll my eyes at my best friend.

"If I didn't, would this little one be here?" Dani says, kissing Remi's nose repeatedly. Our daughter squirms in her arms, and I swoon at the image of them. Snap out it, Nat. She's here for Remi only. It was one night I was nothing more.

"So how big is it? Like this big?" She makes a pea-size with her fingers. "Or like...?" She makes a big gap between her hands.

I smack my friend's arm.

"I..."

"Don't... you don't have to answer that, Dani," I say with an embarrassed smile. She nods and returns her attention to our daughter. She seems to not be interested in Bae or me, instead more with Remona. I pinch my friend's arm.

"Ow, what the hell?" I turn her around to face the sink.

"Stop acting like an ass," I whisper under my breath.

"What... I'm just trying to get to know her. She's in my god baby's life... out of nowhere."

"Asking about her dick size is not trying to get to know her." I give her a dead pane face. She raises her hands in defense.

I look at the clock, and Bailey and I are both teaching a teens class in 5 minutes. I can hear the chime of the door downstairs opening and know the kids are filing in.

"Whatever." She says, grabbing a banana off the counter and walking back to the door. "Nice meeting you."

"You too." Bailey walks out, and I'm left standing there.

"We have a class. Do you mind watching her? I pumped last night. There are a few bags frozen in the freezer if she gets hungry."

"Are you sure you should be working?"

I grab a banana and walk to the door. "I'm fine. Like I said a million times. You are here because of Remona. Not because of me. So could you please just... focus on her."

"I..." She opens her mouth then closes it nodding her head. "Sure."

She stands up, and I watch from the door as she goes to the kitchen, looking into the freezer for the baby's milk. I sigh and walk out of the house, feeling like an ass once again.

CHAPTER 6

February 22, 2023

Dani

It's been two weeks since Remona was born. I'm back at work now but don't really want to. Nurse Johns offered me maternity leave to be there with Natalia, But Natalia doesn't want me there. She's expressed that more than once. So, I took the hint and only helped when she needed. I text her every morning and night to see if I can do anything to help out. And each time, I get a "No. I'm fine, Thanks" It's like her signature words. I get she's fine, but I want to be there for Remi. I haven't seen her in 3 days. Mainly because I went back to work.

For the first week, I focused on Remona like she asked. I was taken aback by her request but nonetheless obliged. I would help keep her house clean and watch the baby while she went to work and took mid-day naps.

She insisted I go back to work this week and that she would just bring Remona down to the studio. I don't know how she was able to work three days after labor. Women are miraculous. Some bounce back sooner than others, but in the end, they are all strong.

I got the results back, and Remi is 100% mine. Not that I ever doubted Natalia. I trust her completely, plus the baby looks just like me. I knew from the second I walked into her hospital room that it was my baby.

"Ay Mamacita, how's motherhood?" Maria says, walking into the nurse station taking a seat next to me. I'm relaxed, leaning back in the chair with my ankle resting on my leg and tossing a happy sac in the air.

"Fine. I guess."

"Why I guess? ¿Es porque la mujer no te dejan en su cama?" (Is it because the woman won't let you into her bed?)

"¿En serio María?" (Are you serious, Maria?) "No, I don't care to get into her bed. But Natalia won't ever let me just worry about her. The woman was up working like she didn't just give birth. Like she doesn't need anyone. I commend her for having that mindset. But everything with her and me is only about Remona. Which I guess is fine... I just wish..."

"She'd allowed you in? Open up? Allow you to get to know her?" I don't even have to say the rest of my sentence for Maria to know what I'm thinking. She's my best friend for a reason. We met years ago at a house party in high school. We were both seniors, but she was new in town, and a guy tried to roofy her drink. I caught him and protected Maria. We made a pack to never go out to parties, clubs, anything mainly without each other. She became my best friend, and we have done everything together.

Same college, same major, same degree and certificates, same job and hospital. The only thing we didn't do together was become parents. And that might have happened together if I had wrapped it up 9 months ago.

She has always known I was intersex. But she and I never saw each other as more and will never. Maria is more like a sister to me. She is just my annoying best friend that has stuck by my side after all these years.

"Yeah. That." I say, finally responding to her. "I want to get the know the mother of my daughter."

"So get to know her."

"¡Puta! I am trying."

"Really dick. When was the last time you saw your daughter?"

"Four days ago," I say, annoyed.

"That doesn't look like you're trying. That looks like you're giving in to her telling you it's strictly about Remona. So if you want to get to know her, push harder. As questions." I groan and toss the happy sac at her. It hits her in the titty, and she yelps.

"Hija de puta" (Motherfucker)

"Watch your language, Nurse Reyes." Nurse Johns says, walking past us.

"Yeah, watch your language. There are tiny ears on this floor," I say mockingly.

"This is your fault. Whatever. Go check on bed 6. Her light is going off." I roll my eyes and stand up, walking to the room with the new mother.

I enjoy my job. I love getting to help the little humans come into the world. They are the most precious little things. But I can't help but only want to be with my daughter right now. I miss her so much.

I know Natalia is doing well, but I'm not sure how to tell her I'd prefer to stick around and possibly stay a few nights to help her out.

Only Platonically. Simply to see Remona and possibly get to know her better. It's as if she's blocking me out and purposefully not asking for help, despite the fact that she claimed from the beginning that she didn't want to do this alone. As if finally meeting me and putting a face to the woman who got her knocked up was enough for her. She hasn't contacted me in three days and only responds to my texts asking if she needs anything. Any more than that, and she'll remain silent.

Does she want to co-parent or not? I can't simply walk in and demand to see my daughter. She carried Remona for nine months and then pushed her out. According to the law, my daughter is primarily hers. And, based on what I've seen, she's not an unfit parent. Not that I would get the law involved. I'd just do what she says and be disappointed that I won't be able to see my baby.

Work ends, and I clock off shift allowing the next nurse to clock in. Maria and I have the late shift, which is typically 3:15pm - 11:45pm. We can change it if we like, but we enjoy this shift since we used to be partiers. So staying up to 12am is never really hard for us. Plus, I get the mornings to myself, which I enjoy.

"Buenas Noches. Te amo mi Hermana" (Good night. I love you, my sister) Maria says, kissing me on my cheek. She hugs me tightly, knowing I need it.

"Te amo. See you tomorrow."

I make it to my apartment and toss my keys in the tray next to the door. I hop into the shower and wash the day away. I wash my long dark hair and scrub my body. After wrapping the towel around my body, I blow dry my hair and brushed my teeth. I finish drying off before putting some boxers on some basketball shorts and a top for bed. I already ate for the night, so I don't do that; instead, I hop in bed and pull the cover-up to my chin.

I don't usually go to bed right after work. Most times, I turn the tv on and relax until sleep takes me. Which is what I do. As I'm finally drifting off to sleep, my phone begins to ring loudly, jolting me awake.

I groan, reaching over and looking at the time. It's almost 2 am. I see it's Natalia, and I rub my eyes, answering the call.

The first thing that fills my ears is the ringing sound of my daughter crying. "Dani?"

"Yeah, Everything okay?"

I hear her sigh heavily. "No, not really. Every night around this time, she cries for hours... and I don't know what to do. She won't stop, and I'm tired. And frustrated, and... I need your help."

I sit up in bed and try to force my body awake all the way. "Okay, I'll be there in a minute."

"Thank you."

"Of course." She hangs up, and I stand up, stretching. I grab a bag putting a few things in it. My scrubs for tomorrow. My toothbrush, hairbrush, boxers, sports bra, socks, and my work shoes. Oh, and my deodorant. I'm not sure if she'd want to stay until the sun comes up, but I want to be prepared just in case. Infants are hard in the first couple of months.

I drive to her house in the dark. Texting Natalia to let her know I'm here so she can unlock the studio door for me. I collect my bag and exit the car, waiting for her at the door. I see the hall light turn on through the window and her approaching the door. She unlocks it and waves me in. I stand there, waiting for her to re-lock the building. She looks at my bag but says nothing; instead, she walks past me back up the stairs.

I notice she's getting better at walking up them. From the stairway, I can hear Remona crying. I dread it when she cries. It makes me sad. As someone who works on a baby floor, we can distinguish the difference between each cry. Some indicate hunger, while others suggest a burp, gas, or discomfort. Her cry is louder, more powerful, and higher in pitch than regular crying. It's almost as though she's screaming.

I place my bag down when she lets me inside the house. Remona is in the grey portable bed I bought the first week.

"Hey, bebita. What's all this fuss for?" I ask, picking the newborn up. Her cries don't die down.

"Yeah, she won't stop crying. It lasts for hours. I give her milk, change her diaper. I'm not sure what to do?" I can hear the plea in her voice. It's normal for her to feel like this. I glance around the house and notice all the lights are on.

"Turn the lights off for me." She looks at me confused, and I take a seat waiting for her to do it. Natalia turns all the lights off, and the only thing bright enough to shine some light is the moon and street lights through the window. I kick my shoes off, place a leg on the sofa and turn how I'm sitting. I shift the baby, so she is face down on the couch. I gently turn her neck and begin to massage her back gently. Soon her cries begin to calm down, and I hear Natalia sigh next to me.

"How...? I Have been trying for days."

"She most likely has colic," I answer, still rubbing our daughter until she drifts to sleep.

"What is that?"

"It is a period of prolonged and excessive crying or fussiness. It's pretty frequent in healthy babies until like 3 to 4 months."

"So I didn't do anything wrong?" She says, sitting on the coffee table, placing her head between her knees. I finally get to take a glance at her. Her hair is wild, and she is in a pink nightgown. I chuckle and lift Remona placing her head against my shoulder.

"No, you didn't do anything wrong. She is okay. The darkness helps soothe her. Try keeping her in the dark when it happens. She seems to respond to a back massage." I chuckle again, realizing I could use one of those to get to sleep too.

I walk towards her room, noticing the blanket for Remi on her bed. I lie the baby down and swaddle her tightly before lowering her into the crib.

Natalia stands in the doorway, watching me. I stand up after kissing Remona's forehead. Walking back to the living room and grabbed my bag and shoes.

"Now that you know how to soothe her when it happens... I guess I should be heading home now." She doesn't say anything, and I take that as my que to leave.

"Wait..." She says as my hands reach the doorknob. "It's late. Why don't you just stay the night? If you know, you might have work or something in the morning. I don't want you wasting time driving all the way back."

"... okay," I say, placing my bag back down.

"I'll get you some pillows and blankets."

I nod and take a seat on the sofa. She brings them to me. "Thank you"

I get comfortable and notice she's watching me from her bedroom doorway again.

"Sorry. Goodnight." She says anxiously and turns around, closing her door slightly. There is a gap between her door and the frame, and I almost feel like she is still watching me. But I don't say anything; I just smile and am grateful she finally called for help. Plus I got to see my daughter again.

Chapter 7

February 23, 2023

The smell of pancakes and bacon filled my nose as I rubbed my eyes awake. I slept. It wasn't the best sleep because it wasn't in a bed, but it was good enough because I finally got to see my daughter after three days. Even if it was only for a few minutes to calm her crying.

I roll over, making sure not to fall off the couch, and look towards the kitchen. I see Natalia still in her nightgown from last night. Or rather this morning when I came over. Her hair has been brushed, and she's wearing house slippers. I notice a blanket over her right shoulder and her using one arm for cooking. So I'm assuming Remona is under the blanket in her arms eating.

I don't get why she tries to cover herself when feeding our daughter. I see breasts all day at work... and vaginas. I'm an RN for the OB floor. Plus, I've seen her breasts, granted it was over nine months ago, but still. Maybe she's just self-conscious. I don't know why. She has a beautiful body. She turns around and catches me staring at her, and I turn my face to cover my blushing.

"Why do you always look at me like that?"

"Like what?" I say, yawning and grabbing my bag.

"Like I'm a piece of meat."

"You aren't, and I don't. Just.... admiring my daughter's mother, that's all." I say lowly, walking to the guest bathroom to wash my face and brush my teeth. I brush my hair and twist it into a bun before turning off the light and walking back to the kitchen.

I walk towards her, and she stands there in front of me awkwardly. I flash a smile. "Is she done eating?" I ask excitedly. I don't think I'll ever get over being a mother or having a tiny human that's mine. She lifts the blanket and looks down at the baby passed out with her nipple hanging out of her mouth. I smile at the milk dripping down her chin.

"She's out. You can have her." She says, pulling her nightgown back up and lifting Remi to me. "She woke up a few times this morning to eat."

"Why didn't you wake me? I would have just made her a bottle and let you get some sleep."

She shrugs. "Because I know you have work today. And I don't, so I didn't mind letting you get some rest."

"I told you I'm here to help. I don't go to work until 3 pm."

"Yeah, I know..."

"If you know, why are you refusing help from me?" I ask, annoyed, sitting on a stool at the kitchen island. She turns back to the stove and continues to cook.

"I'm not refusing your help."

"Yeah, okay, whatever."

She puts a plate of food and a cup of orange juice in front of me, and my annoyance deteriorates. "So you work downstairs or?"

"Yes, and I own it. It was my mother's studio for 20 years. When she and my dad died in a car accident three years ago, it was put into her will for me to have."

"I'm sorry about your parents. That must have been tough." She stands there with food on her plate, leaning over the counters. She pushes her scrambled eggs around, and I glance down at Remona squirming in my arms before going back to sleep.

"It's okay," She finally says. "It happened a while ago. It was hard at the time. I went through the stages of grief, but I bounced back from it. I miss them a lot, but... there's nothing I can do about it now." I stare at her. "What?" She asks, chuckling with a gorgeous smile on her face.

"What what?" I say, taking a sip of my juice.

"You're looking at me like I have two heads."

"No. I'm just surprised you're finally opening up and talking to me." She rolls her eyes, but her smile still stays.

"There's just a lot going on, Dani. Everything is still new to me."

"Yeah, I know that, but you don't have to shut me out. I'm here for the both of you. I still want to know the woman I accidentally knocked up." Her face turns red, and she continues to eat as it goes silent between us again. "So were you a dancer before getting the studio or just picked up the teaching."

"I've been dancing at this studio since I was four. My mother put me in her classes. I danced all the way up through high school and then went to the art academy down the street. When I got my degree in dance, I followed in my mother's footsteps and took up her studio."

"Was that your dream?" She nods her head.

"One hundred percent. I've loved dance since I was a little girl, but I always sucked with the jitters when it came to the competitions. Hated the mini panic attacks I'd get before each meeting."

"That's cute," I say, bouncing Remi in my arms.

"It's not. It's embarrassing."

"I don't know. I've never really had stage fright or been afraid to get up in front of a crowd."

"Well, let's hope Remona gets that gene."

"I don't know. I think she'll steal the spotlight from every room she walks into like her mother." I see that all too familiar blush and she stands up straight, putting her dish in the sink.

"Are you done?" She says, reaching for my empty plate. I nod, and she begins to wash dishes.

"Don't. Here take her. I'll do them." She is hesitant at first but moves out of the way.

"You don't have to clean up every time you're here. You know?"

"Yeah, but I enjoy it."

"You like cleaning?"

"Yeah, you don't?" I don't know why I ask. Her house was a total mess when I first came. Clothes everywhere. Dishes not done. I mean, I get she was living alone and pregnant and still working. So I don't fault her.

"I mean, I don't like a mess. But it's difficult to clean sometimes." I nod, understanding. Which is why I don't mind helping out. "Thank you." She whispers, walking towards her room. "I'm going to get her ready for a bath."

I rush to get the dishes done because I want to be there. Every little thing dealing with Remona I want to be a part of if Natalia will let me. After drying my hands, I walk and stand in the doorway of her bathroom. She's still small, so we don't bathe her but every other day. And I've never been there for any of them, including the one at the hospital. I watch as she kneels on the outside of the tub and washes Remi in a small separate container inside the big tub.

She looks back at me and smiles. "Do you want to wash her?" I match her smile and nod. Rolling my sleeves and kneeling next to her. She scoots over, and our daughter sits there making noises that don't resemble anything but babbling.

She sits on the floor, bringing her knees up to her chest, and just watches me bathe Remi. "So, what about you?"

"What about me?" I ask, glancing her way.

"Are your parents still alive... Remona's other grandparents."

"Yeah... but I don't talk to them as much."

"Oh...why?" I drain the tub and Pick up Remi. Holding her in a warm towel. Natalia follows me back into her room as I place the baby down on the bed.

"After I hit late puberty around 15 and found out I was intersex, we kind of got into a heated argument. They felt like them deciding to choose my gender for me at birth was the right thing to do... I felt like it was selfish of them. For years I felt something was off with me. I had a penis and testicles, yes but... at one point... I had a vagina and ovaries. And though there are a ton of medical problems that come along with having both. I understand why they chose for me. But the least they could have done was tell me they made that decision. It would have shed some light on why I had such bad gender dysphoria early on."

She was laying on her stomach on the bed with her feet dangling behind her and her chin resting on her palms. She stares down at Remi, but I could tell she was listening to me. I glance behind her at her nightgown riding up and feel my stomach turn. I quickly go back to dressing Remona in a grey onesie for the day, looking at the time and seeing I still have about 2 hours before I have to go to work.

"I get that. Do you still talk to them? Or after the argument, that was it?"

"I still talk to them every once in a while. Make sure they're doing okay. And they do the same for me. It's very cordial between us. I don't spend holidays or anything with them. I mostly spend my time and holidays with Maria. Plus, my parents are divorced."

"And you and Maria?" She's getting more comfortable asking questions, and I like it. I am an open book to her and have nothing to hide.

"She's just my best friend. We've known each other since high school."

"Yeah, that's Bae and me." She says quickly.

"Mmmm, So no, you and Bailey?"

She chuckles, playing with Remona's feet. "No. Definitely not, She has a boyfriend."

"Okay... just checking."

"Why?" She asks, quickly looking up to me.

I just shrug and pick Remi up, walking out the room.

"Don't try to hit on me, Dani. I'm not gay."

"Ahhhhh? Is that so?" I asked, placing our daughter in the rocker.

"Yes, that's so." She quickly follows after me, sitting on the couch. Again her gown rises, and my eyes instantly go to her thighs. She notices and pulls the fabric down. "I'm not gay." She reiterates.

"That's not what you said the night we hooked up."

"I was drunk."

"You were sober enough to understand you were dancing with some-one with a dick and breasts. You felt it when we were dancing, don't deny that. And you made the sober decision to stick with me the rest of the night."

"I didn't deny it was there. And yes, I did decide to dance with you..."

"Aht and go back to the hotel and hook up." She grabs a pillow and tosses it at me.

"Shut up." I catch it laughing and putting it next to me as I grab my stuff needed to get ready for work.

"I'm just saying. straight, gay. bisexual, pansexual, asexual... the list goes all. But they are all just labels. Love is love regardless of what is under a person's clothes."

"Whatever. It's not love. It's a preference, and mine isn't... you." I nod my head a little disappointed and stand up, waving my things.

"Do you mind if I go shower in the guest bathroom, I have work soon?"

"Ahhh... yeah, sure."

As I walk away, I can feel her eyes on me, but I don't bother to turn around. I waste no time showering and getting ready for work. When I head out into the living room, I notice she and Remona aren't there anymore and hear the tv on in her room. I don't say bye. I guess you can say the comment still stung. Instead, I just grab my things and head to the front door, opening it and locking it from the inside. The studio is full of kids when I get downstairs, and I see Bailey teaching a class. She waves with a smile, and I do the same back before heading to my car and going to work.

CHAPTER 8

A pril 9, 2023

Natalia

In the early morning light, I wake up to the soft whines of Remona. We find ourselves co-sleeping, a practice Dani warns me against due to safety concerns, yet I simply can't resist. She is my baby, and an overwhelming desire to keep her close to me at all times tugs at my heartstrings.

Her tiny hands reach for me, grasping the fabric of my shirt with surprising strength. She tugs, a signal I've come to understand over these past two months. As I lift my shirt, she latches on almost instantly, her wide eyes never leaving mine.

Today is her first Easter, a thought that sends a flutter of excitement through me. With every little milestone like this, it becomes more and more real - I'm a mother. In public outings like today, I usually pump a few bottles beforehand, despite knowing that breastfeeding is a natural and normal thing,

There's a comfort and a connection here that words fail to describe. Yet, the public eye seems so judgmental, so critical. I find myself pumping more often than not when we go out, the fear of disapproving glances too much to bear. At home, though, it's different. Here, I can nurse her without worry, without fear. This is our safe haven, a place where she can feed freely, and I can relish the closeness.

It's just us two at home, and at times like this, I feel the void left by another adult presence more deeply. There are times, in the quiet of the night when Remona is fast asleep, that I crave for someone else.

Someone to share in these beautiful moments. Someone to laugh with, to confide in. To reassure me that everything will be fine and that I am doing everything right as a mother. I yearn for the intimacy of an adult connection. I long for someone who would wake up next to me, someone who would be utterly in love with me.

Before I had Remona, my life was different. I'd date casually, enjoying the company of different people, never wanting anything serious. I loved my body and embraced my independence. But since becoming a mother, I've retreated. I've cocooned myself in the new role, nervous about stepping back out into the world that seems to have moved on without me.

With a sigh, I gently lower Remona from my chest, settling her onto the bed. She protests, her tiny face scrunching up, but soon settles back to sleep. I search through her dresser for her clothes while she is resting.

Dressing Remona for the day feels like a sacred task. Today is a special day, and I want her to look just as special. I carefully choose a light, airy cotton dress, white with pastel-colored Easter eggs scattered across it.

To give a touch of Easter bunny spirit, I choose a matching pair of bunny ears. They are soft, pink, and fit snugly onto her tiny head. As I gently guide her small arms through the sleeves of the dress, she jerks herself back awake. Her eyes dart around before allowing her hands to mindlessly swat the bunny ears off her head. The moment she gets ahold of them, it goes straight into her mouth. I chuckle, watching her enjoy the new texture against her gums.

With my baby looking absolutely adorable in her Easter best, I lay her down on her two-months milestone blanket. It's one of those ones that has each month up to a year marked on it. I arrange the soft, pink bunny ears to form a circle around the '2', framing it nicely, before grabbing my phone for pictures.

"Okay Remi, look at Mama. Yes, that's it, good girl!" My finger clicks away as I capture my little girl in her Easter ensemble. Each click is a memory stored, each photo a promise of stories to tell her when she's older.

I send off a quick text to Dani, attaching the best pictures of Remona. The reply comes back almost instantly.

"Mi conejita." [My little bunny.] Her following text brings a smile to my face, "I'll be there in an hour. Would you like me to pick up breakfast?"

I look at the time and realize I've not even showered yet, let alone cooked breakfast. "I don't feel like fast food. Don't worry about me. See you in an hour." Placing Remi back into her crib in the living room, I rush to the shower, grabbing her baby monitor to watch her eyes slowly close again.

I've barely turned off the water when the smell of breakfast hits me. Confused, I wrap a towel around me, water still dripping from my hair as I step out of the bathroom.

The sight that greets me leaves me momentarily stunned. Dani, in my kitchen, cooking. She looks at me, a playful smile on her lips, "I thought you said an hour."

I made her an extra set of keys, one for the front door of the dance studio and another for my house. Considering she's here quite often for Remona, it seemed like the sensible thing to do. But never did I expect her to thoughtfully break and enter to prepare me breakfast.

"I know," She turns her attention back to the stove. "But you didn't have time to cook so I rushed over to make you something before we leave."

I find myself locking eyes with her, caught in her radiant smile, and for a brief moment, I forget about everything else. But the thought of us going anywhere near 'that' route scares me and I break the gaze, suddenly feeling self-conscious in my towel. Mumbling a quick thanks, I rush back to my room to get dressed, the smell of breakfast making my stomach rumble in anticipation.

As we sit in silence at the kitchen island, the aroma of breakfast flows through the air, filling the room. I find myself quietly grateful that she hasn't revisited our previous conversation about her not being my type.

The scent of freshly brewed coffee and sizzling bacon lends a comforting atmosphere, soothing the potential tension of the morning. She looks from Remona to me, a question forming on her lips. "What was your Easter like growing up? She asks, her voice barely more than a whisper.

I hesitate for a moment, my mind flooded with memories of my parents. It's still painful to think about them, but also comforting in a way. She must see the conflict in my eyes. "You don't have to talk about it, Nat."

"No, it's okay," I say, smiling at her calling me Nat for the first time. "I actually like remembering them."

She leans back in her chair, giving me space to open up at my own pace. I draw in a deep breath, thinking back to those cherished memories of my childhood. "We used to go to the Catholic church every Easter. It was a big thing for us. After the mass, we would stay for the festivities. There were egg hunts, games... It was a lot of fun."

Her eyes soften as she listens. "Did you continue the tradition after..."

I shake my head, the memory of my anger towards God still vivid in my mind. "No. After they died three years ago, I stopped going to the church. I was angry at God for taking them away from me."

"And now?" Dani asks, her voice barely a whisper.

I look down at my hands, a wistful smile tugging at my lips. "I never went back to church. But I did talk to God, in my own way. Made up with Him, you could say." I let out a small chuckle, the irony not lost on me. I was able to find comfort in my relationship with God without needing the formal setting of the church, which was where I first connected my faith and my parents.

"But going back to the church..." I trail off, my eyes drifting toward Remona. "It holds too many memories of them. It's just too painful."

Dani simply nods. It grows quiet before a smirk washes over her face.

"So you grew up in a Catholic Church huh?"

"Yeah, why?" I match her smile.

"No reason."

"What? Spit it out." I shove her playfully and she chuckles shaking her head.

"Nothing. It just makes sense." She picks up our plates walking them to the sink.

"What does."

"You." She starts to wash the little number of dishes left.

"Me?"

"Mhm, everything about you just clicked."

"How?"

"Let me guess... CCD classes on a weekday after school?" She is speaking of the Confraternity of Christian Doctrine which are religious education programs for children in the Catholic Church.

She glances back at me waiting for my response. I cover my mouth trying not to laugh but shake my head no. Her eye widen questioning.

"Pre-k to 12th at Our Lady of..."

"I knew it!" She cuts me off and I can't help rolling my eyes laughing.

"What? Your parents didn't put you in private school or CCD classes."

She nods. "CCD yes. But I made peace with my faith in knowing it accepts me for who I am."

I squint my eyes at her, confused by what she means. "My faith accepts me for who I am."

"Mhmm I..." she's cut off by Remona's cries from the crib and wipes her hands off before walking from the kitchen to our daughter and picking her up. She looks at the clock and kisses the side of Remona's head. "We should probably start heading to the event now."

I nod in agreement, gathering our things as she continues to comfort Remi. She heads to the front door, opening it for me with a faint smile. "After you."

"Thank you," I reply, the words rolling off my tongue before I can stop them. I watch as she locks up, her movements efficient and familiar.

She reaches to help me with Remona, her fingers brushing against mine as she takes the car seat from my hands. She's gentle as she buckles her into the base in the back seat of her car. I take a moment to watch them, a strange sense of warmth blooming within me. She opens the passenger door for me. I offer a brief smile in return, whispering a soft 'thank you' under my breath.

The drive to the local park is quiet. The earlier conversation about my parents and Easter traditions still hanging in the air between us. We don't talk much, but it's not uncomfortable.

We arrive at the local park just as it starts to fill with families. I glance at Dani, noticing the twinkle in her eyes. She's looking at Remona, her gaze full of warmth. A subtle fluttering stirs within me again, a response I quickly dismiss.

We set up a mini egg hunt for Remona. Obviously, at two months old, she's not going to be scurrying around collecting eggs, but we create a small, colorful display around her blanket. Dani snaps away on her phone, documenting her first Easter. As the day progresses, we engage in simple games, ones that mostly involve Dani making funny faces to make Remi squeal. I find myself caught in her orbit, my eyes lingering on her more often than I care to admit.

She's so natural in these moments, effortlessly fitting into the role of a mother. She's patient with Remona, careful not to let the excitement overwhelm our little girl.

The day moves along, filled with light-hearted activities. We take Remona to the little petting zoo set up at the park. Dani holding her tiny hand against the soft fur of a bunny. I snap a picture, capturing the pure joy on their faces. It's another one for our growing collection of family photos. Family. It's an interesting term, one I hadn't thought to apply to us before.

But just as soon as the thoughts come, I squash them down. The image of us as a family, while comforting, is also terrifying. The implications it carries, the potential changes it could bring to our dynamic - it's all too much to consider. So, I ignore the warmth spreading through me, brushing it off as nothing more than the result of a good day.

And yet, as we pack up to leave, I can't help but steal one last glance at her. For the first time, I allow myself to truly see her, not just as a friend or Remona's other mother, but as a woman. The realization is subtle, but it's there, lingering in the back of my mind. I push it aside for now just focusing on the here and now - Remona's first Easter, a day filled with love, joy, and just a tiny bit of confusion.

Chapter 9

A pril 12, 2023

Natalia

Two months and four days. That's exactly how long it's been since I gave birth to my baby girl. At this point, she's discovered her little hands, trying to grasp at everything within her reach. Particularly her favorite toy, the rainbow teething ring.

Since Easter, things between us have changed subtly. The dynamic has shifted, and though I can't pinpoint whether it's due to our conversation about her 'not being my type' or my admission of being raised in a church, I can't ignore the fact that Dani's been distant. She still cares for Remona with the same love and devotion as always, but there's a reserve in her laughter now, a hint of strain in her smiles.

Tonight, I am venturing into unfamiliar territory. I'm going on a date, my first since becoming a mother. But it's not with Dani. The thought crosses my mind and I quickly dispel it. I couldn't – wouldn't – go on a date with a woman. Yet, I can't deny the surge of conflicting emotions swirling within me, and it's not entirely about the impending date.

In this moment I yearn for an intimate connection with another adult, a craving that's been intensifying lately. I'm just longing for a simple, honest connection, a balm to soothe the loneliness that comes from long nights and days filled with motherly duties. It's an urge, a need for companionship that doesn't just revolve around diapers and baby toys, but shared laughter, common interests, and mutual attraction.

A part of me questions whether this date is about more than just filling a void. Or an attempt to escape the confusing whirl of emotions I've been grappling with. It's a thought that gives me pause, making me question my motives. Yet, I quickly dismiss it, not wanting to dive too deep into the pool of uncertainty.

I'm standing in front of the mirror, nervous anticipation curling in my stomach. I scrutinize my reflection, looking at the woman who's evolved from carefree to cautious, from spontaneous to meticulous.

As I gaze at myself, the reflection peering back at me seems distant. My fingers trace the line of my waist, flit over the stretch marks adorning my skin – remnants of carrying Remona. My beautiful baby girl, her existence now my entire world.

I decide on a little black dress – it's simple, classy, a remnant of my pre-motherhood wardrobe. The dress hugs my body, revealing the new curves that motherhood bestowed on me. I turn sideways, examining myself. My fingers absently tug on the hem, and my mind wanders to Dani.

The soft crackle of the baby monitor from the bedside table interrupts my chaotic thoughts. I glance toward the source, and my breath catches as I pick up the device. The screen lights up with the image of Remona fussing in her crib, her soft whines vibrating through the silent room.

I watch as the nursery door opens on the monitor and in walks Dani. Her silhouette is a familiar, comforting sight, one that has graced many of our late nights and early mornings.

I watch as she lifts Remona from the crib, her arms cradling our daughter with practiced ease. Her soothing whispers, inaudible through the monitor, work their magic. Remona quiets down almost immediately, her little head tucking against Dani's shoulder.

Who is Daniella to me? I find myself pondering this question more often these days.

She's Remona's mother - something we'd never planned on happening, yet somehow we find ourselves here. She's there through every sleepless night, every first-time-mother panic, every moment of sheer joy watching Remona reach a new milestone.

And yet, there's more. There's this strange pull I feel toward her. It's in the way her presence brings comfort and stability. It's in her quiet strength, her soft smiles, the warmth that seems to radiate from her. It's something I've never experienced before. It confuses me, this unfamiliar emotion, this uncharted territory.

I am not gay. That's a fact I've known my whole life. I like men. And yet, here I am, unable to dismiss the undeniable charm of this woman. But I can't go there, can I? I've spent the last few months since Remona's birth navigating this new life. I've grappled with so many changes, and this... this is not a complication I'm ready to explore.

But, for now, I'm going on this date. It's just dinner with a man. I glance at the clock – it's time. My date, a man named Josh I met through a dating app, is waiting outside.

As I step out of the room, I find Dani in the living room, holding Remona in her arms, whispering sweet lullabies that float through the air, bringing a sense of calm. Her eyes meet mine, and she smiles, a soft, genuine smile that lights up her face.

"You look amazing," she says, her voice holding a note of something I can't quite place. It's not the first time she's complimented me, but this time, it feels different. There's an undercurrent there that wasn't before.

"Thanks," I reply shyly, a rush of warmth spreading through my cheeks. It's strange the way my heart flutters at her words. I try to ignore it, attributing it to the anticipation of the night ahead.

As I turn to leave, Dani's voice stops me in my tracks, "Are you sure about this?"

I look at her, surprised by her question. "About going out on a date?" I ask, trying to keep the irritation out of my voice. Why should she be worried about what I choose to do with my personal life?

"Yes," she says simply, looking at me with that unnerving, gentle concern. I used to say it was looking at me like I was a piece of meat. But I know it's not. She's always had the uncanny ability to make me feel seen, even when I don't want to be.

"I'm sure, Dani," I say more forcefully than I intend. I don't need her concern or her worry. Or at least that's what I keep telling myself. "I can handle a date."

"Just...take care of yourself tonight, okay?" Her gaze is intense, full of apprehension. It's not just a generic farewell or a friendly piece of advice. It's more personal, more profound.

"Of course, Dani," I reply, a tad irritated at her needless worry. "I can take care of myself."

I know she's referring to the date, to the dangers of the city at night. But the way she looks at me, her eyes full of emotion, makes me feel like there's more to it than just physical safety. It's as if she's asking me to be mindful of my feelings, my heart, like she's afraid I might be treading on thin ice emotionally. The idea is absurd. I'm just going out, trying to move on with my life, like any other single mother would. Yet, as I turn away from her, her words echo in my mind. But I shake them away as I leave for the date.

The evening has gotten off to a good start, but I'm not sure how long it will last. Josh, the man sitting across the table, carries himself with an assured air of confidence. His life, as he narrates it, is a whirlwind of high-stakes finance, adrenaline-pumping adventures, and an unexpected flair for culinary arts. Yet, as he effortlessly hops from one exciting tale to the next, I can't help but feel the soft pull of yearning for my little Remona.

"In Tokyo, I found this old sushi master who took me under his wing," he recounts, his hands illustrating his tale. He's animated and lively as he relives the memory.

"That must have been a fantastic experience, Josh," I reply, steering my thoughts away from my daughter. I've left her in Dani's capable hands; I know she's okay.

Josh's gaze turns back to me, his curiosity piqued. "What about you, Natalia? I'd love to hear more about what you love."

Caught off guard, I mull over my response. Can I admit that my recent passion is motherhood? Can he comprehend the fulfillment I draw from nurturing my little one? But the curious gleam in his eyes prompts me to play it safe. "Well, I love music, literature... and my work, of course. I'm a dance teacher."

"Dance, huh? That's intriguing. Ever since I got back from my mountaineering expedition in the Himalayas," he interrupts, effectively veering the conversation back to himself.

As the evening wears on, I find myself slipping into a rhythm of polite nodding and feigned interest. Josh is charismatic, sure, but his seemingly endless tales of self-glorification gradually grow tiresome. But tonight, I'm playing the dating game again after a long hiatus, and for now, I'm bearing with it.

When our main course arrives, I'm jolted out of my musings. The expertly prepared dish in front of me is difficult to appreciate as a familiar sensation begins to draw my attention away.

My breasts ache, a warmth spreading through them that has nothing to do with the atmosphere of this date. I cringe inwardly, realizing I had forgotten to pump before leaving, and now it's Remona's feeding time. My body is painfully in sync with her schedule.

"Excuse me, Josh," I say quickly, standing from our table and hurrying toward the restroom. The physical discomfort is impossible to ignore, my body's urgent reminder that Remi's needs don't pause for my personal life.

Once inside the bathroom, I pull out my phone. My fingers fly over the screen as I open the app connected to the baby monitor at home. The screen comes to life, showing Dani feeding her a bottle, her gaze tenderly fixed on our daughter. A lump forms in my throat, a mixture of relief and regret.

I groan softly, tipping my head back to stare at the bathroom ceiling. I'd much rather be at home right now, feeding Remona and discussing mundane day-to-day things with Dani. Yet here I am, on a date I don't even want to be on, dealing with dampness and discomfort in a restaurant bathroom.

Pushing the longing aside, I concentrate on tending to the immediate issue at hand. I clean myself up as best as I can, using the heat from the hand dryer to help dry my dress. I take a few extra moments to touch up my makeup and smooth down my hair. I give the peaceful scene on my phone one last look before I steel myself, pushing away the regret.

When I return, a look of concern washes over Josh's face. "Everything okay?" he asks, his brows knitting together.

I force a smile, trying to keep the mood light. "Yeah, it's just... new mom stuff, you know."

A smirk crosses his face, his gaze lingering just a tad too long on my chest. "Well, motherhood certainly has its... perks." The words hang in the air like a bad joke. I swallow back my distaste, feeling my earlier nerves replaced by a newfound discomfort.

The rest of the date passes in a blur of awkward conversation and forced laughter. As Josh drives me home, he continues his monologue, recounting his every achievement. The car pulls up to my studio, and the engine hums in the silence.

"Well, Natalia," he starts, leaning in, closing his eyes in anticipation. I brace myself for the inevitable end-of-the-date kiss. But before he can close the distance, I put a hand on his chest, stopping him in his tracks.

"Josh, I...I had a good time tonight. But let's call it a night, okay?" I manage to get out, stepping out of the car and into the cool night. Relief washes over me as I close the door behind me, leaving behind the heavy cloud of my first date post-Remona.

Returning home, the soft glow of the living room light guides me to a sight that stirs warmth within me. Dani is curled up on the couch, Remi nestled against her chest. The hush of the TV playing in the background provides a comforting soundtrack, its volume turned down low enough not to wake our sleeping daughter.

Silently, I discard my coat and shoes and make my way to them. Her eyes flicker towards me, a quiet welcome in her gaze. The sight of them, so peaceful and content, eases some of the night's residual tension.

"How was the date?" she asks, her voice barely above a whisper, careful not to disturb Remi.

I shrug, sinking into the adjacent armchair. "Josh was...okay, I guess."

Her eyes linger on me, studying my expression. I can't quite read her. Is that relief I see? Disappointment? It's hard to tell.

"Just okay?" she prompts, her brows arching in a silent question.

"Yeah. He talked a lot. About himself mostly," I admit, unable to keep the frustration from seeping into my voice.

She hums sympathetically, her thumb gently stroking Remona's back. "Sounds exhausting," she comments, a hint of something akin to satisfaction coloring her tone.

"Yeah, it was," I say, leaning back and closing my eyes. The soft babble of the TV lulls me, offering a soothing end to an otherwise chaotic evening.

Chapter 10

April 15, 2023

Dani

The hospital's cool air hits me as I step inside, the feeling of comfort and familiarity seeping into my skin. It's my birthday, though I've kept that bit of information to myself. Natalia has had enough on her plate without needing to worry about me. Especially after that weird date, she went on a few days ago. The thoughts have been eating away at me, though I remind myself, it's none of my business.

She hasn't wished me a happy birthday, but why would she? I'm just a co-parent to our daughter. Last night, I texted her, asking if I could have Remi for the night so I could celebrate my birthday with the one person I truly wanted to be with. However, her response was a simple, "Sorry, she's with Bae for the night. I have plans." I know that the "I have plans" text probably means she went out on another date, and I shouldn't let it bother me as much as it does. Why should it matter to me who she spends her time with?

What upsets me more was that she didn't even give me the option to pick up my daughter or visit Bailey's place to see her. I didn't want to create any tension between us or make things awkward by reminding her that today was my birthday. I mean, I didn't want to go all out and bang pots and pans or scream it to the world. However, back at the hospital, when she asked me to enter my passcode, I did tell her it was 0415—my birthday.

I had to lower my expectations of hoping she would remember. I did remember hers, not that she ever told me. But I did invasively read her chart on the day she gave birth to Remi, with the sole purpose of learning more about her.

I find myself remembering such small details about her. Like how she struggles to put her clothes in the dirty hamper. Leaving them in mountains, on the floor, next to the basket. Or how she sulks when it's time to do the dishes. Which is why I always take care of them when I'm around.

I notice the way she furrows her brows when something puzzles her. Or how she strategically avoids her vegetables, trying to camouflage them with more appealing options because she knows they're important to eat.

I am mesmerized every time she counts Remona's tiny toes and fingers as if our daughter still possessed the same enchantment she had on the day she entered this world. Which... she does.

Even when she's in her dance studio, I find myself captivated by her. I occasionally visit with Remona just to appreciate the mother of my child and demonstrate my interest in her, even if it's just a little.

The mere thought of her brings a smile to my face. The way she moves with such grace, guiding her ballet students with a gentle yet firm hand. Her strength and her stubborn determination to make the best life possible for Remona. All these things draw me to her, pulling me in like a moth to a flame.

I see the way the mothers at the studio watch me. They're kind, friendly, some even flirtatious. I can't seem to return their interest. In my mind, there is only space for one person, and she had occupied it entirely. Yet I've taken up none of hers.

Stepping into the nurse's locker room, I'm met with a burst of colors and an eruption of cheerful "surprise" from the nursing team. Maria is at the center, her wide grin a sight.

The locker room had undergone a total makeover, decked out with decorations that instantly brought a surge of joy. Colorful streamers hung from the ceiling, swaying and dancing with every breeze. Bright balloons, dressed up with shiny ribbons, adorn the ceiling, and there is a "Happy Birthday" banner and signs plastered across the walls. It's a complete transformation from the dull lockers to a vibrant space of celebration, and I have my over-the-top best friend to thank for this.

"¡Feliz cumpleaños, puta!" Maria shouts. (Happy birthday, bitch!)

"Oh, you're just too kind," I respond sarcastically, grinning back. "You didn't have to do all this." I look around the room, letting my hand run across the party streamers on the ceiling. Other nurses come by, patting my back and wishing me a happy birthday. I'm thankful for it all; it makes me feel special, a stark contrast to how I was feeling before.

"I bet Natalia wished you a happy birthday," she nudges, her eyes twinkling with mischief as she watches me. I take off my shirt, standing in just my sports bra. I put on some deodorant before grabbing my scrub top.

"Actually, no, she didn't. And that's okay. It's not like it's a national holiday or something." I smirk, my hands fumbling with the buttons of my uniform.

"See, that's your problem," she retorts, her eyes never leaving my face. "You always downplay everything, even your own birthday. I bet if it were Remona's birthday, you'd make it a national holiday."

I chuckle, shaking my head at her accuracy. "You're probably right," I admit, tugging my scrub top down into place.

"You probably don't even have plans tonight, do you?" she asks, her tone laced with disbelief. I shrug.

"Maybe, maybe not. Who's to say?"

"Want to go to the club?" She wiggles her eyebrows.

"The club? No, Maria. We don't get off until damn near 1 am." I drop my shorts to my ankles, kicking them off. Now standing in just my boxers. She rolls her eyes and groans, sitting down to put on her shoes.

"Yeah, but it's the perfect time to go then."

"Puta, you'll pass out before we even get there. Besides, I don't need it ending like the last time."

"Oh, you mean with a sexy baby mama?" She stands quickly, shimmying in my face. I shove her away, and she smacks her teeth.

"Yeah, one that gives me no time of day and sees me only as a co-parent to our daughter. Anyway, aren't we supposed to be working?" I purposefully steer the conversation back to safer waters.

She gives me a knowing look but doesn't press further. "You better at least have cake. It's not a birthday without cake."

I let out a sigh of resignation as I shut my locker, and we walk out of the locker room together.

The day begins with a quick handover, where the day shift nurses share vital information about the patients in our care. As we discuss each woman's progress, I can sense the energy building, knowing that some may be just moments away from the miracle of childbirth.

I check my assignment for the day and find that I'll be assisting in the delivery room again. I make my way to the room where a woman named Sarah is in active labor. Her partner, David, is by her side.

"Good evening, Sarah... David," I greet them warmly. "How are you feeling today?"

She smiles through her contractions. "Evening! I'm feeling a bit anxious but also really excited. Can't believe the day is finally here."

I nod empathetically. "It's completely normal to have mixed emotions at this stage. But as we discussed previously, we're here to support you every step of the way. So, let's revisit your preferences. I recall that you wanted a natural birth with minimal intervention. Is that still your preference?"

Sarah nods but soon exhales with discomfort. "I'm feeling a bit tired, and the contractions are getting more intense. I might be considering pain management options. What are my choices?"

"You have a few options. We can start with non-medical techniques like breathing exercises, relaxation techniques, and different positions to help you cope with the contractions. How does that sound to you?"

Sarah considers the options for a moment. "I've been practicing my breathing techniques, but I'm unsure how effective they'll be as the pain intensifies. What are some additional options available if needed?"

I acknowledge her concern. "One option is nitrous oxide, also known as laughing gas. It's self-administered and can help take the edge off the pain during contractions. It's safe for both you and the baby, and it wears off quickly. Another option is an epidural, which involves the administration of local anesthesia to numb the lower part of your body. It provides more significant pain relief but can limit your mobility."

She looks at David, seeking his input. "What do you think? I'm not sure which option would be best for me."

He takes her hand and offers his support. "Sarah, it's ultimately your decision. We'll support whatever choice you make."

She nods. "I think I'd like to try the non-medical techniques for now, and if the pain becomes too overwhelming, I'd be open to exploring the option of nitrous oxide first."

I nod and document her decision in her chart. "That sounds like a good plan. Remember, it's okay to change your mind at any point and opt for different pain management options. Our priority is to ensure your comfort and safety. I'll be here to guide you through the breathing techniques and assist with any additional comfort measures you might need. You're doing great."

She smiles, feeling reassured. "Thank you, Dani."

As the labor progresses, Sarah's contractions intensify, and she expresses her fears about the pain. Eventually, she decides to get the epidural. There's no judgment from me—I watch women push these babies out every day, and it looks gruesome to see a big-headed baby come out of such a small hole.

I hold one of her knees, and another nurse has the other. "You're doing amazing, Sarah. Each contraction brings you one step closer to meeting your baby. Take it one moment at a time, and we'll be right here with you."

David interjects, his voice filled with pride and love. "Sarah, you're the strongest woman I know. We're in this together, and our little one is so lucky to have you as their mom."

She squeezes his hand. Finally, reaching the pushing stage. The OB prepares for delivery, and I position myself to assist. Together, we guide her through the process, encouraging her with each push. The room fills with anticipation and excitement.

"You're doing incredible," The doctor says. "Just a little more."

She grunts, her face flushed with exertion. Her baby emerges into the world with one final push, and the room fills with cries of joy.

"It's a boy!" Is announced, holding the newborn up for them to see.

Sarah's voice trembles with emotion. "Oh my God, he's perfect."

I place the baby on her chest, encouraging skin-to-skin contact.

After cleaning up and allowing the parents to have some precious moments with their baby, I sink into the chair at the nurse station, feeling the weight of the day settle upon me. Maria, joins me, smacking on a chocolate bar. Catching her eye, she asks, "How was it?"

Leaning forward, I carefully grasp a delicate blue bead and gently place it into our designated baby jar. Blue signifies a boy, pink a girl, and white represents the painful loss of an angel baby. While such occurrences are fortunately infrequent, they still happen more often than I would prefer.

Witnessing a family bear such heartbreak remains the most challenging part of my job. Additionally, we reserve purple beads for intersex babies or those who do not conform to society's standard expectations, although these instances are even rarer than angel babies. Nonetheless, it's important for us to keep track of every precious life.

"Exhausting. I'm ready to go home," I mutter, feeling the weariness sink in.

She gets excited, clapping her hands before digging into a bag that's hidden under her shirt. She pulls out a very small single cake with the biggest grin on her face. I notice what kind of cake it is and roll my eyes.

"Maria, you stole that from Caydence."

"Shut up! Candy will be fine."

"I heard that," Caydence says, walking past us. She gestures the 'I'm watching' fingers. "You owe me a cake, Maria."

"Yeah yeah, Candy, you'll get your cake." She grabs a lighter and sticks a candle she found in the break room drawer. It's a single candle for a single cake. "Your birthday isn't over yet, mi hermana. To your big 25."

I softly smile and lean forward. "Wait." She stops me. "Make a wish first."

I sigh, closing my eyes and wishing only to watch my daughter grow up and be there for every milestone. I blow the candle out, and before I can do anything else, she smashes it into my cheek.

She bursts out laughing before licking my cheek. "Ewww, puta. I do not know where your tongue has been."

"You wish you knew."

"We will never!" I push her head away and grab a few napkins to wipe the leftover cake from my face.

The remaining hours are quiet, no more birthdays happen. No more babies being born. Beyond the clinical aspects, I have the opportunity to engage in conversations with new mothers, providing guidance and support during their stay. We discuss breastfeeding techniques, share stories of sleepless nights, and celebrate the small victories that come with parenthood.

Yet, between the multitude of interactions with patients, my thoughts involuntarily drift back to Natalia. Even as I witness the bare and sometimes demanding nature of childbirth, her presence lingers in my mind.

chapter 11

A pril 29, 2023

Natalia

I'm dropping Remona off at Dani's today, which is rare. An almost nonexistent occurrence. It's not that Dani's apartment is far from my studio—quite the opposite —but it feels as if I'm crossing an unspoken boundary.

I'd done this countless times, handing Remona off to Dani for their time together, but I'd never actually been inside her place before.

Pulling up to the unfamiliar parking lot of her apartment building, I kill the engine and check the rearview mirror. I see Remi nestled cozily in her car seat, her enchanting dark brown eyes brimming with curiosity.

With gentle care, I release the buckle and lift the carrier from the backseat, cradling the precious weight of her existence in my arms. "Let's go see Mommy, Rem," I whisper, brushing my fingers lightly over her soft cheeks, causing her to break into a gummy grin. Her tiny fists wave around, her enthusiasm infectious.

I click the carrier into the stroller, ready for our little trip. We navigate the sidewalk to Dani's apartment building. Entering the lobby, I maneuver the stroller toward the elevator, pressing the button with a soft 'ding.' I look down at Remi, her eyes fixed on the changing lights of the elevator panel.

"All right, sweetheart. Hold on tight. We're going up."

As the elevator chimes our arrival, a small pulse of anxiety throbs within me. Walking down the unknown corridor, I approach her door and knock gently, the rhythmic tap echoing my unease. It's not long before the door swings open, and Dani stands there, her silhouette outlined by the warm light of her apartment.

There's a fleeting moment. One where our eyes lock, and we stand in silence. There's a noticeable tension between us. A quiet discomfort that has been building gradually.

It wasn't always like this. The first time Dani ever came over for Remi, we were a sort of a forced united front. Two people tethered together by our love for this tiny human. She used to show genuine interest in my life, asked about my day, my likes and dislikes, dreams, and fears. I wish I could say I reciprocated. Eager to learn every detail about this woman who was the other mother of my baby. But I wasn't, and a small part of me still isn't.

Yet, as the days passed and I began dating again, the dynamic between us seemed to subtly shift. Her smiles felt more forced, our conversations started to dwindle, and our bond seemed to be slowly eroding. I don't know if it was the dates that triggered this change or if it was something deeper, something hidden beneath the surface of her polite smiles.

As I step inside, I note the artistic minimalism of her apartment. Everything is neatly organized, each item thoughtfully placed, yet there's a simplicity that hints at a single woman's lifestyle.

I find my gaze straying towards the right, where a door left slightly ajar offers a tantalizing peek into a room filled with a riot of color. Every stuffed animal, book, and toy has a designated place, yet they're clearly loved and well-used.

Dani's salary as a nurse, which is decent in our city, allows her to comfortably afford this two-bedroom apartment. The thought momentarily distracts me. Her hard work and dedication have clearly paid off, creating a warm and inviting home for her and Remona.

Even as I take in the details, I realize that her life is neatly compartmentalized, much like this apartment - organized, clean, with a place for everything. Yet I can't shake off the feeling that, like these rooms, there are still areas of her life that remain inaccessible to me, hidden behind closed doors. I'm not sure if it's my fault or hers. Sometimes I wish I could look through those doors and truly comprehend the woman who is an equal part of my daughter.

This silence between us feels like a gap widening with every passing day, despite our shared responsibility of raising Remi. It's strange how we seem to be moving in opposite directions instead of forming a cohesive co-parenting unit.

She seemed genuinely interested when I told her about my first date. She'd asked questions, smiled, even joked a bit. But as the dates have become more frequent, I sense her withdrawing, drifting away like a boat unanchored. I can't pinpoint whether it's the dating or something else entirely, but the chill of her silence is undeniably noticeable.

As she free Remona from the snug confines of her car seat, her soft voice fills the air. "Hello, Remonita, How was your night with Mama?" she coos.

The baby responds with an endearing scrunch. Her tiny body curly inwardly. Her delicate arms and legs draw closer to her chest as if cherishing the comfort and security of her mother's embrace.

"oh, that's a big scrunch, isn't it, mija." She babbles back, her small hands reaching out as if trying to grab hold of Dani's soothing words. She's growing so fast, her personality shining brighter each day.

The colicky, sleepless nights are a distant memory now. Our baby girl sleeps peacefully, her dreams undisturbed by the fussiness that once kept us awake at ungodly hours.

While Dani focuses on Remona, I take a moment to absorb the surroundings. I tear my gaze away from the intimate exchange, my eyes wandering around the apartment as I slowly circle the room. I feel Dani's eyes on me, her gaze warm but quiet, as if trying not to disrupt my exploration.

The apartment is a mirror of her personality, every corner an intimate detail about her. A shelf is lined with an array of intriguing books. Various picture frames are scattered around, each snapshot a slice of her life - a laughing Dani in front of the Grand Canyon, another of her graduating with a radiant smile, another of her cradling Remi as a newborn, the love evident in her gaze.

A small vintage record player occupies a corner, and an assortment of vinyl records sits next to it - The Beatles, Nirvana, Miles Davis -

music tastes as diverse and intriguing as Dani herself. Yet, there's so much about her that I still don't know.

Each item tells me more about her than she herself ever has. The old photographs, the worn-out running shoes by the door, the journal with its edges slightly frayed. It's a life I have been so close to, yet I've always been standing on the sidelines, afraid of what stepping into it might mean.

I'm aware of the importance of wanting to know more, of wanting to dig deeper. It could lead to something that feels dangerously close to intimacy, something that I have been consciously avoiding.

A 'Happy Birthday' card on the table attracts my attention. It is distinct from the structured chaos that surrounds it. I notice it just as Dani is bouncing Remona around, attempting to get her to produce the most recent sound of laughter. Her undivided attention was on our daughter. However, the card acts as a magnet, drawing my gaze to it.

"Whose birthday was it?" I ask, my voice breaking the stiff air between.

I pick up the card, my fingers tracing over the handwritten notes, signatures, and well wishes. All the names are familiar - the delivery team from the hospital where Remona was born. And then the date - April 15, 2023.

A moment passes before the realization dawns. It was Dani's birthday. Two weeks have passed, and I forgot Dani's birthday. I should have kept in mind her passcode, 0415, but I didn't. How could I ever forget the first time she revealed herself to me as an open book? A book that I've yet to crack open and one that she's stopped offering glimpses of.

"Dani, I... I didn't realize..." I begin, but words fail me. She simply shrugs, trying to downplay the situation, but I see a hint of disappointment in her eyes. She was hoping that I'd remember, that I'd acknowledge this important day for her.

There's a deafening silence that follows. I didn't even let her see Remona that day. I had Bailey watch her while I went on yet another disastrous date. I have to apologize. But what words could possibly make up for this? This woman has shared a life-changing experience with me: bringing our daughter into the world. And I just ... forgot.

"Dani, I'm so sorry. I... I should have remembered," I stammer, my voice barely above a whisper. My apology is raw and sincere.

She responds with a simple, "It's okay," but her voice says otherwise. She's hurt, though she does a good job of hiding it. I watch as she turns her attention back to Remona, pulling her into a light game of peek-a-boo that has our daughter giggling.

She lifts Remi, smelling her bottom. "Let's get you changed, stinky butt."

Left alone in the living room, I find myself letting out an involuntary groan, pressing the heels of my palms into my closed eyes. I carefully place the card back on the table as though it's an artifact loaded with regret. I follow the muffled sounds of their interaction to where they disappeared.

Standing at the threshold of Remona's room, I take a moment, my gaze drinking in the riotous bursts of color and life contained within its four walls. She is gently changing Remi, her eyes filled with excitement. Observing them in this shared space, I hesitate, almost unwilling to intrude.

From her position, Dani lets out a chuckle, her hands skillfully managing Remona's squirming form. "You can come inside, Natalia. It's not the Pentagon," she jests. I smile as my name playful rolls off her tongue.

Despite the invite, I still feel like I'm intruding into their shared space. "I didn't want to interrupt," I counter lightly; my gaze roams around the room, lingering on every toy, every storybook—each piece seems to narrate a snippet of Dani's and Remona's personalities, their shared world that I'm just beginning to understand.

Just as I'm about to speak, Dani beats me to it. "Has she had tummy time today?"

"Uh, no, not yet."

As if on cue, Remi is promptly turned over, a bright toy waved before her. I can't help but admire the ease with which Dani maneuvers these simple routines. I'm aware she works with mothers and newborns on a daily basis, yet it's different when it's your own. Did it come to her as naturally as it seems, or is it the outcome of years of experience and exposure? Is it instinct or practice? These questions remain unanswered as I watch her interact with her daughter.

Then, almost unexpectedly, she breaks the silence again. "What time do your dance lessons end today?" she asks, never once lifting her gaze.

My eyes glance at the clock on the wall. "Around six."

"Do you want me to bring Remi back to your place tonight?" Her tone is nonchalant, businesslike, as if we're just two colleagues discussing a project, not two mothers navigating our way through co-parenting.

I chew on my lower lip, contemplating. This is what I wanted, isn't it? To be strictly parents, nothing more? "No," I finally utter, "she can stay the night."

Her gaze shifts to me, probing. "Is it because you have a date?"

Rolling my eyes, I counter, "No. Most of them haven't gone well. Might I add?"

Her snort echoes in the silence that follows. "What's so funny?"

Shrugging, she replies cryptically, "I wonder why."

"What's that supposed to mean?" My tone is sharper than I intended.

"It just seems like you're looking in the wrong places." Her words carry a deeper meaning than they suggest, an undercurrent that leaves me flustered.

Feeling defensive, I retort, "I think I'm doing a great job getting back out there."

She just smiles, noncommittal, leaving me uncertain and slightly irritated. "I guess."

Annoyed now, I grab my purse, "I'll leave you two to it then." I sling my purse over my shoulder and step out of her apartment, leaving behind the riot of color that is Remona's room and the quiet, enigmatic presence of Dani.

CHAPTER 12

M ay 8, 2023

Natalia

The cool morning air brushes against my skin as I approach the two graves that bear the names of my parents - Nalida and Carlos Lopez. Today is my third birthday without them, and the absence of their love, their presence, has been the hardest part of these years.

"Happy birthday to me, huh?" I whisper to the wind, wishing it could carry my words to them wherever they are. I can almost see the image of my mother's hands carefully bringing out a double chocolate cake, big colorful numbers standing proudly on the top. My father, with his warm smile, asking me to make a wish before blowing out the candles.

My fingers trace the carvings of their names, a tangible reminder of a loss that time hasn't healed. With a sigh, I take a seat on the ground and lean forward, carefully pulling out the weeds that had sprung up since my last visit.

"Mami, Papi," I begin, my voice shaky. There's an intimacy in talking to them, even in their absence, that I find comforting.

"I miss you both so much," I confess, my heart heavy. The silence of the cemetery allows my thoughts to echo, bounce around, and fill the space where responses used to come.

"I'm a mother now. Her name is Remona, and she's the most beautiful thing I've ever seen." I swallow hard, the words catching in my throat. "I never thought I'd become a single mother, much less out of marriage."

A pause. The breeze blows softly, rustling the leaves in the nearby trees. "I wonder, would you be disappointed in me?" I ask, my voice a mere whisper. "Because I have a child with another woman? Because I'm raising her in a broken home? Because I didn't follow the path, you expected me to?"

I take a deep breath, "Mami, I need your help... am I doing a good job? Being a mother? I wish you were here to guide me, to give me advice. I feel so lost sometimes."

My heart pounds in my chest as I broach the subject, I've been wrestling with for weeks now. "And then there's Dani..." My voice trails off, my mind filled with images of her, of us. Of the growing feelings that I've been trying to suppress.

"I think...I think I might have feelings for her," I admit to the silent gravestones. "But I don't know what to do with these emotions. I've always believed in what the church taught us about love, about marriage. But now... now I don't know what to think."

I let the silence envelop me, a chilling reminder of the void my parents' absence has left. "Would it be wrong, in the eyes of God or in your eyes, if I acted on these feelings?" I ask, looking at the stones as if they could provide me with answers.

"I'm trying to be strong, for Remona, for me. But it's so hard." The tears fall freely now, the pent-up emotions finally breaking through the dam.

"I hope, wherever you are, you're not disappointed in me," I whisper, wiping my tears, straightening my shoulders. "I hope you're proud of me."

Time slips away, marked only by the peaceful current of the wind and the shifting shadows. Eventually, I rise to leave, replacing the old, wilted flowers with new ones. Before I go, I kiss two fingers and place them tenderly on each tombstone.

The drive home is filled with quiet contemplation. Today is a day I've kept free every year, canceling my dance classes in honour of the day that now bears a different weight.

Remona is with Dani. It was only fair, wasn't it? After all, I had left Dani alone on her birthday, unintentionally, but the fact remains.

Pulling into the empty parking lot of the studio, I find comfort in the familiar routine. As I approach the studio door, reaching for the handle, the lights flick on in an instant, and a chorus of "Surprise!" envelops me. Blinking in shock, I step back, nearly stumbling as I take in the sight before me.

My dance studio has been transformed. Streamers and balloons in a riot of colors adorn the room, a 'Happy Birthday Natalia' banner draped across the wall. There are familiar faces from my dance class, all gathered around a table piled with presents.

"What in the...?" I murmur, standing still in amazement.

I stand in the doorway for a moment, absorbing the sights and sounds of the surprise birthday party. Everyone sends waves and smiles in my direction but quickly returns to their conversations once the initial surprise fades.

From the crowd, Bailey emerges with a drink in hand and a mischievous smile playing on her lips. "Happy birthday!" She yells, handing me the drink.

"Bailey, did you do all this?" I ask, scanning the room.

She shakes her head, her curls bouncing with the movement. "No, it was all Dani," She corrects me, her eyes sparkling with a secret I hadn't been privy to.

"Dani? Really?" I echo, the shock evident in my voice. "She put so much thought into this. And I... I forgot her birthday." The guilt, previously tucked away, resurfaces and tugs at my conscience.

Bailey merely shrugs, her lips curving into a knowing smirk. "Yeah, I know. Surprised me, too, when she shot me a text to contact all the dance moms and students. If you don't jump on that, Nat, I will."

I let out a faint laugh, playfully shoving her shoulder. "Jeffery would kill you."

"Jeff knows I'm all his," she counters, turning her head to flash a cute wave at her boyfriend, who was busy with a group of dads.

I roll my eyes, shaking my head at her antics. "Right... and I'm not jumping on anything."

Her smirk turns more serious, and she leans a little closer. "You seem to be jumping into a lot of dates recently." Her tone is teasing, but I can sense the hint of concern beneath.

I can't help but glare at her comment. She's my best friend, so she's allowed to cross certain boundaries. I shrug nonchalantly, deciding to brush off her comment. "I'm just looking."

She nods, her eyes thoughtful. "Yeah, in the wrong direction," she mumbles into her drink.

My brows knit together in confusion, irritated by her vague words. It's like an echo of what Dani's said before. Have they been talking about me to each other? I groan, "What is that even supposed to mean?"

She doesn't answer me immediately, taking a long sip of her drink instead. "Nothing, Natty. Just... Your faith is important, but it shouldn't force you to deny your true feelings."

Before I can respond, Bailey is moving away, leaving me with her words. A swarm of dance moms quickly take her place, all of them wishing me a happy birthday and sneakily hinting at the gifts they got me before I even get to open them.

The party surges around me, the dance studio filled with the lively rhythm of music and the cheerful chatter of guests. Children, my little dance students, scamper around, their faces glowing with un-restrained excitement.

Suddenly, a dance mom raises her hands, quieting the room. "We have a special shared gift for Ms. Natalia," she announces, her words sparking an eager buzz of anticipation.

The children group together at the center of the room, ready for their performance. Their eagerness shines in their eyes as the music shifts to a softer, rhythmic tune, and they start their dance. Their movements flow in beautiful synchrony, their faces lighting up.

As they dance, my eyes find Dani in the crowded room. She's seated, with Remona on her lap, moving our daughter's little hands in beat with the performance. She catches my gaze from across the room. A soft smile graces her lips, a simple, tender gesture that sends my heart racing. Feeling my cheeks heat up, I quickly avert my eyes just as the dance routine concludes to enthusiastic applause.

Immediately after, the children swarm me, begging to open their gifts. They excitedly show me their presents, pointing out which one is theirs and what wrapping paper or bag they've chosen. I glance around, searching for Dani, but she's nowhere to be found. I spot Remona with Bailey and Jeffery, but Dani remains elusive.

My thoughts scatter as the room begins to fill with the melody of 'Happy Birthday.' The crowd parts, revealing Dani carrying a double chocolate cake, a colorful 25 sparkling on top. She reaches me just as the song finishes.

"Make a wish?" she offers, her voice almost drowned by the excited cheers. I close my eyes, make a wish, and blow out the candles during the resounding applause.

"How did you know I like double chocolate?"

She shrugs, nodding towards my best friend. "I asked Bailey."

I mouth a 'thank you' to her, to which she nods. The moment is broken as the kids crowd around us, their eager faces looking up at the cake like it's the most magical thing they've seen.

As the party carries on, Dani keeps her distance. She talks to other guests, plays with Remona, or retreats to secluded corners to feed our daughter. Despite the noise and activity, she manages to get our cranky baby to nap. I watch her, taking in her laughter, her carefree demeanor, and the ease with which she mingles with the guests.

Eventually, I see her heading my way, Remona cradled in her arms, sleeping, her face serene as she navigates the crowd. As they get closer, I try to look casual. But on the inside, a flurry of anxiety takes hold, like a thousand butterflies fluttering in my stomach. She reaches into her bag and hands over a gift to me.

"We made this for you," she says, her voice soft.

"We?" I ask, my heart thumping against my ribs.

With trembling hands, I unwrap the gift; the paper crinkles under my fingers as I peel it off. Inside the box, nestled in layers of pastel tissue paper, is a photo frame. I lift it out delicately, my heart now in my throat. The picture inside captures a precious moment from Easter – it's me, holding Remona high above my head. Her tiny face is lit up with an enormous smile, her joy as bright as the sun that day.

"Oh, this is...thank you, Dani. This means a lot," I manage to say, fighting back tears.

Before she can respond, a small interruption comes in the form of a young girl tugging at my dress. "Ms. Natalia," she says in an urgent tone. "There's no more tissue in the bathroom for Chloe."

I open my mouth to say I'll handle it, but Dani beats me to it. "Don't worry about it," she says, giving me a reassuring smile. "Enjoy your party. I've got it."

With that, she slips away, leaving me standing in the midst of the celebration. The rest of the party continues with laughter and music filling the dance studio. But my mind is elsewhere, constantly trailing after her, even as I find myself carried along by the celebration around me.

It's not until the party starts to wind down and everyone leaves that I finally find the courage to approach her. It's just her and I and Remi. She's busy cleaning up the dance studio, picking up discarded decorations and plates. "Need some help?" I ask, my voice steady despite the turmoil inside me.

She nods but moves across the room to clean another area away from me. Her smile isn't as bright as it was in front of everyone. It's like when it's just us alone, she holds her tongue.

The rest of the cleaning goes by in an awkward silence; the only words exchanged are me telling her where to dispose of the garbage. When we finally finish, She prepares to leave, walking upstairs to the house and gently placing our daughter in my bed.

I grin at where she put her. "I know you're co-sleeping." She says, shaking her head, amused.

"How could you possibly know that."

She rolls her eyes dramatically at my reaction. "She gave up her crib at my place weeks ago. Refused to sleep unless she was in my bed."

I cross my arms, "How do you know it's my fault?"

Her gaze flickers to the living room, and the answer is clear as day. "Her crib hasn't moved from that spot in weeks. If she was sleeping in it, it'd be next to your bed. Where I originally put it, because I know you need her near you to sleep properly."

"So?" I challenge, not ready to admit defeat.

Laughing softly, she picks up Remona's blanket from my side and swaddles her snugly before setting her on the crescent-shaped pillow next to mine. "So, Natalia. You can not sleep without our daughter. And she can not sleep without our presence... because of you. Hen ce... you are co-sleeping."

"You caught me." I pout.

"Just be cautious, okay?" I know she's wary because it elevates the risk of SIDS and suffocation. Believe me, the fear of every little thing that could potentially harm my baby constantly looms in my mind. But it's hard; I just can't sleep without her.

I nod, and she walks past me to the living room to gather her things. "I'm going to head home."

Standing at the threshold of my bedroom, I internally beg her not to leave, knowing I would never actually say it out loud. "Thank you for today... everything else aside." I add, subtly referring to my guilt over forgetting her birthday, even as she made mine so special.

She doesn't answer just continues to navigate my living room to find her things. At last, she ceases her motion, and before I realize it, she's standing right in front of me. Her eyes blink slowly, and a faint smile forms on her face. "Of course," she murmurs, her voice gentle, a feather-light sound in the stillness between us. She leans in, planting a soft kiss on the side of my cheek. "Happy birthday, Princesa," she whispers, the words lingering in the air as she steps away, moving towards the front door.

I touch the spot where her lips met my skin, the warmth of it still there. The door closes gently behind her - she never is one to slam the door. Yet, as if on cue, Remona's cries fill the silence, as though the door had crashed shut. It seems our little one has an acute sensitivity to her mother's absence, and so do I.

CHAPTER 13

May 20, 2023

Dani

The warm hum of conversation and the soft tapping of ballet slippers against polished hardwood are the first sounds I hear as I enter the dance studio. I'm once again armed with a box of sugar-glazed treats, hoping to brighten the Friday evening of a bunch of hard-working little dancers.

Standing off to one side, I observe Natalia leading her young charges through a series of intricate dance moves. She notices me watching her and points towards Remona's crib, nestled in a quiet corner.

Remi's in the middle of one of her midday naps, a precious slice of peace in her otherwise energetic day. I tip-toe over to the crib, careful not to disturb her. I could easily take our daughter and leave, but I know that moving Remi would only disturb her sleep and mess up the carefully orchestrated nap schedule we've established.

As I settle next to the crib, my phone in hand to pass the time, I realize I've let go of any lingering disappointment about Natalia forgetting my birthday. It happened. It's in the past. My sadness was more of an interior state than an outward display, but I eventually got over it. We have many more years ahead of us, bound together by our connection to Remona.

Despite her lapse about mine, I wanted hers to be memorable. After all, she's Remona's mother, and her birthday also marks the day we conceived our daughter, even if both of us barely recall that day in its entirety.

Class eventually begins to wind down. Natalia rounds off the session with a cheerful announcement, "Ms. Dani has brought donuts for everyone again!" The children's tired faces brighten up with excitement when they hear this.

A wave of chatter washes over me as a group of tiny dancers rush my way. I open the box and watch as their eyes widen at the sight of the sweet treats. This has become sort of a Friday tradition, my appearance with a box of donuts marking the end of their practice session and the start of the weekend.

One by one, the children flock to me, their little hands reaching into the box, their small fingers grasping the donuts. They thank me, their words rushed in between bites. I watch them savor the donuts before they eventually leave, their parents calling them away.

I look back to the box, seeing one lonely donut left. That's strange. I always make sure to buy the exact amount for the children. My eyes scan the room, finally landing on Tiffany, a small figure still sitting in the corner of the studio, her hands working to untie her ballet shoes.

I glance at Natalia, hoping she would notice that a child is still left behind. But she's engrossed in her phone, texting with a smile, oblivious to the situation. "Tiffany," I call gently, catching her attention. She looks up, and I beckon her over. As she approaches, Remona stirs awake. I lay her on her stomach for tummy time, placing a toy in front of her, giving Tiffany my full attention.

"Where's your mom?" I ask.

She shrugs, her shoulders lifting in a nonchalant gesture, "I think she's on her way."

Deciding to fill the time, I ask, "What have you learned so far?"

The question piques her interest, and she takes a step back, ready to showcase the moves she learned. Her performance starts with a delicate technique where she bends her knees while keeping her heels firmly on the ground. "Plié," She says, her voice ringing with pride as she names the move.

Next, she does something I've seen countless times in their classes. She leaps from one foot to the other as if she's bounding over an imaginary obstacle. The word escapes my lips before Tiffany can voice it, "Pas de chat."

She doesn't correct me, just nods with a smile and moves on to the next position. She extends one leg behind her and balances perfectly on the other. Her arms reach out to create a straight line with her extended leg. "Arabesque," she chimes, maintaining her balance.

I applaud as she finishes her routine, a wide grin on her face. Just as Tiffany ends her performance, the door to the studio swings open with a ding.

Wendy, Tiffany's mom, rushes in. Her face is slightly flushed, her breaths coming out in small huffs. Her hair, a vibrant red, is cut into a short bob that swings as she walks. She's dressed in a white blouse and navy blue slacks, an outfit that screams casual yet professional.

"I'm sorry I got held up at work. My last customer's dye took forever to set," she explains.

"Customer?" I ask, intrigued.

"Oh yeah. I'm a hairdresser, and turning a brunette into a blonde right before closing? Nightmare. Takes a long time to lift," she says, running a hand through her perfectly coiffed hair.

I nod in understanding. "My mother is a hairdresser as well. She's been doing it for over 20 years."

"That's neat. I'll have to ask her for a few tips and tricks sometime," Wendy replies, a small smile playing on her lips. Our eyes hold each other's gaze for a moment longer, the silence only broken by the sound of something falling nearby.

Natalia's voice cuts through the air. "Shit, sorry. Just me dropping the speaker."

The moment broken, Wendy turns her attention back to her daughter. "Well, thank you for watching her for a few more minutes. Again I'm sorry I was late."

"Want me to show you the dance moves we learned today, Mommy?"

"Um, no, sweetie, that's okay; you can show me when we get home. Let's go and get some dinner first. Thank you again, Dani," She says, her attention now on me.

After moving a few steps away, she abruptly halts and spins around to face me again. A hopeful twinkle lights up her eyes as she suggests,

"Would you consider grabbing a bite to eat with me sometime? I mean... Only if you'd like to, of course."

Caught off guard by her sudden question, I freeze momentarily. It's a date request - simple and casual. Yet, it feels unexpected.

My eyes instinctively flicker towards Natalia, who's been occupied, or rather pretending to be, with tidying up the dance studio. It's as if time has come to a standstill, and the only sound that resonates in the small studio is the rhythmic ticking of the wall clock.

Wendy's innocent question hangs in the air, the words filling the room with a tension I hadn't anticipated. "Oh. No. I'm sorry, I thought you two weren't a thing. Did I get... it wrong?" The words stutter out of her mouth, a blend of confusion and uncertainty.

Natalia remains silent, her back to us, seemingly engrossed in sorting through the endless pile of ballet shoes and dance tutus. I wait for a moment, giving Natalia a chance to say something. But all I get from her is silence.

In the stillness of the studio, I find my voice, the words clear and confident. "We are not a thing. We just co-parent Remona. That's all." The air seems to shift as the words leave my mouth, the tension breaking.

I can now feel Natalia's gaze on me, as though her eyes are lasers burning a hole in my skin. Yet, I don't waver. I don't turn my gaze to meet hers. Instead, I focus on Wendy, who looks visibly relieved. "And yes. I'd like to take you up on that offer sometime."

"Great," She says, her face lighting up with a smile that reaches her eyes. I can't help but notice the adorable snaggletooth peeking out when she grins. She quickly retrieves her phone from her purse, unlocking it, and handing it over to me. I add my number and pass it back to her.

Remona's crying distracts me, her tiny sounds grabbing my attention instantly. The studio, the dance props, the suspense – everything fades away as I turn to tend to my little girl.

"I'll let you go. See you," Wendy says, her voice fading as she leaves. I nod, cradling Remona in my arms,

"Bye, Ms. Dani. Bye, Ms. Nat. See you next week," Tiffany calls out before the door closes behind them.

Natalia's voice breaks the brief quietness. "I didn't know your mother was a hairdresser."

"You don't know many things, nor do you care to ask." I walk away to collect Remona's diaper bag.

"Are you going to go?" she asks, stopping me in my tracks.

"Go where?" I ask, turning to face her.

"On a date with Wendy."

I shrug in response. "Maybe."

"You know she just got a divorce?"

"And what's that got to do with me?" I challenge.

"Maybe she's not girlfriend material."

"And you think you are?" I snicker. My words cut through the air, sharp and biting. My gaze holds hers steady, a challenge echoing in the question, one well-deserved.

"I..." She starts to respond but falls short, perhaps realizing the pointlessness of the argument.

"Right. I don't meddle in your love life; you don't meddle in mine. That's what you wanted, right?" Leaving her with those words, I turn and walk out of the studio, Remona's diaper bag in hand, ending our conversation right there.

CHAPTER 14

July 10, 2023

Dani

"Cabron, shut up!" Maria yells, shoving me and covering her face from embarrassment. "Is she still looking?" She asks, peeking over at a beautiful dark skin woman. "Damn! She has curves for days."

"Just go talk to her." I insist.

"Hell no!" She yells, her lack of self-confidence evident in her response. Despite my efforts to assure her of her beauty and worth, she struggles to believe in herself when it comes to finding love.

It's disheartening to see my best friend hype herself up, building courage and confidence, only to stumble when it's time to talk to someone. We both made a pact that if we reach the age of forty and find ourselves still unmarried, we would embark on a platonic marriage with each other.

Shaking my head, I let go of the thought of our pact and shift my focus back to the crowd, scanning the vibrant streets of Long Beach in search of the specific people who are supposed to be meeting us.

A kaleidoscope of colors and an electric atmosphere sets the stage for one of the most lively celebrations of love and acceptance—Long Beach Pride. Everywhere you look, the air is infused with an undeniable energy.

The streets were adorned with rainbow flags fluttering proudly in the breeze, each vibrant hue representing a different part of the LGBTQ+ community. Laughter, music, and cheers echo through the streets as people of all ages, races, and backgrounds come together to honor their authentic selves.

It is something I look forward to every year.

From drag performers sashaying down the sidewalks in their dazzling outfits to street artists creating masterpieces before your eyes. The stages were alive with a myriad of performances, from talented local artists to renowned LGBTQ+ icons. The rhythm of music pulsated through the streets, inviting everyone to join in, to dance freely and without judgment.

As the vibrant energy enveloped the streets, I find myself sitting alongside Maria, eagerly awaiting the arrival of Natalia, Remi, and Bailey.

Maria and I spent a few hours clowning around at the beach bar. It was just social drinking, sipping on our beverages in moderation. I want to remain fully present and lucid to celebrate my baby girl's first Pride.

While Remona is too young to comprehend the celebration happening around her, I look forward to the day she will grow older and begin to understand the significance of Pride and the importance of acceptance.

I want her to grow up in a world where love knows no boundaries and where she feels proud of her parents' unwavering support for diversity and equality. Yet, for the time being, I wish for my little girl to remain as little and precious as she is now.

"Do I look okay?" Maria asks, adjusting her top. She's trying to look good for the woman she's been staring at this whole time.

"Why? It's not like you have the cojones to go up to her."

"Well, sorry we weren't all born with cojones like you." She rolls her eyes, and I glance down at her outfit.

She wore a pair of form-fitting, high-waisted pants that hugged her curves in all the right places. The pants have a bold and eye-catching pattern which she paired with a sleeveless, plunging neckline blouse that showcased a hint of skin. She knew her outfit screamed confidence, opposite to what her mind screamed.

I, on the other hand, went simple with black shorts and a vibrant shirt with patches representing LGBTQ+ identities.

"You look good."

"Okay, good." She sighs.

Finally, our group appears before us. Bailey brought her boyfriend Jeffery, which was expected, but to our surprise, Natalia brought along a 'friend'—a guy we have never met before. Not that I've met any of her many dates.

Observing them from a distance, I watch as he wraps his arm around her shoulder and whispers in her ear, causing her to giggle. My gaze then shifted to Remi, peacefully slumbering in the stroller pushed by Bailey. Her shirt proudly proclaimed, "My Mommies Love Me."

Nat catches my eye again, and I take in her appearance—her one-shoulder, open-back crop top is adorned in the vibrant hues of the rainbow flag. She has on black shorts that cup her thighs tightly. My gaze stuck a little too long as I appreciate her effortless beauty.

Maria playfully shoves me out of my trance, snapping me back to the present. She smirks mischievously and asks, "What flavor of the week is this?"

I smirk at her comment, shaking my head. "Aww, come on." She says, sitting up straight. "Looks like a scoop of... vanilla bean dream or maybe even plain ol' white chocolate crunch."

"Maria." As they draw closer, I attempt to lower her voice.

She slaps my arm not letting up. "Oh, oh, oh. I've got it! How about snowflake surprise? Or maybe even milky marshmallow swirl?"

We both bust out laughing at her, inventing unusual flavors that sum up the essence of the unknown white man walking toward us.

"Hey, sorry we're late," Natalia speaks once they finally reach us. "This is Liam. Liam, this is Daniella and Maria."

I cringe slightly at her use of my actual name. It's a level of familiarity I don't want this little boy to have with me. I don't know him, don't particularly care to, and I'm sure as hell not comfortable with the idea of him getting to know my daughter. Ignoring their presence, I scooped up my 5-month-old and walk away.

Eager to explore the Pride festivities, I shift Remi in my arms and lead her through the crowd. Pointing out the colorful sights and engaging her with animated conversation. Her baby ear muffs provide protection from the overwhelming noise.

"Look, Remi! Do you see all the colorful flags?" I whisper to her, even though she can't quite hear me. Her tiny fingers reach out towards a fluttering flag, enchanted by the colors waving in the breeze.

"Yes, sweetheart, they're so pretty, aren't they? And look over there! See the people dancing and twirling?" Her eyes widen, her gaze fixated on the dancers, fascinated by their energy.

I gently poke her chubby side to grab her attention. "Oh, and look at that float coming our way." She quickly turns her head, her gaze following the direction I'm pointing. Then, she looks back at me, her little face breaking into a gummy grin, revealing her first tooth that has finally made its appearance. "Ugh, you're so adorable." I pinch her rosy cheeks together and shower her duck-like lips with kisses.

I continue to stare at her noticing the way our resemblances continue to blossom with her growth. Whether it's the shape of her eyes or the curve of her smile, there are glimpses of myself reflected in her features. It's a humbling and beautiful reminder that I have a daughter. Even now, as I hold her close, the reality of her existence still surprises me every day.

Unfortunately, amidst the lively atmosphere, I overhear Liam making offensive jokes about the LGBTQ community. Natalia nervously laughs, reluctant to correct him. Frustration wells up within me, but I choose not to cause a scene.

Cradling Remi in my arms, I sway gently to the rhythm of the Pride festivities buzzing around us. She starts to get fussy, squirming and making soft whining sounds. I glance towards Natalia, her observant eyes already catching the subtle change in Remi's behavior. "Hey, mamas, are you hungry?" she asks softly, reaching out to take our daughter from me.

Once Remi is secure in her arms, Natalia's eyes start to scan the surroundings of the stroller, her gaze darting around in search of something.

"What are you looking for?" I ask, curious about her frantic hunt.

"Her blanket, to cover myself while she eats."

I help her look, but with Remi's crying escalating, our search is in vain.

I look around before remembering Bailey and Jeffrey took it with them on accident when they left to grab some food. "It's okay, Nat. You don't need it."

Her eyes scan the crowd and then return to meet mine. I can see the uncertainty in her wide gaze. "Are you sure?" she asks softly.

Knowing her tendency to feel self-conscious and her preference for covering up while breastfeeding, I offer her a reassuring nod and a gentle smile.

She bites her cheek with hesitation. After a moment of contemplation, she releases a sigh, deciding to let go of her apprehension. With a subtle movement, she lowers her shirt and swim top, exposing her breast and allowing Remona to latch on. Her head bobs slightly before finding the nipple and attaching herself. I admire my daughter, my hand automatically reaching out to gently stroke her head full of hair.

Suddenly, I hear Liam's voice, "You aren't going to cover up?"

I ball my fist, holding back the urge. I look down at his hands, carrying a turkey leg in one and a beer in the other. "Why don't I cover you up while you're eating, asshole?" I retort.

He casually waves his hand towards the crowd, "I'm just saying, there are a ton of people here."

"And I'm just saying my daughter is allowed to eat without some asshole sexualizing her mother's breast," I snap back, rage seeping into my words.

As my anger rises, I feel a gentle touch on my arm. With her calming demeanor, Natalia places her hand on mine, silently pleading with me not to entertain Liam's idiocy. I jerk my arm away from her grasp, trying to shrug off the anger simmering within me. "Nat, deal with your flavor of the week, please."

Maria grabs my hand, pulling me away from the situation and directing my attention back to the ongoing parade. Letting go of the escalating tension, I refocusing on the celebration surrounding us.

We joined the others after the parade, heading towards the beach to bask in the sun for a few more hours before we have to head home. During the walk, we engaged in conversations, getting to know Bailey and Jeffrey better.

Maria and I struck up an interesting discussion with them while Natalia and Liam seemed to be lost in their own world. I try to let go of earlier events despite Natalia's occasional glances in my direction, reminding me.

Upon reaching the beach, Bailey and Jeffrey playfully run towards the water, throwing sand at each other. Maria lays out a beach blanket for all of us, providing shade with an umbrella to protect Remi from the sun.

Liam breaks his conversation with Natalia, turning to me. "I'm going to grab us a drink," he states as if we were interested.

Maria and I exchange a look, silently questioning why he's bothering to tell us when we couldn't give two shits. We both smirk, reveling in the unspoken dialogue coursing between us. Snickering, we shrug off his announcement and settle comfortably into the beach chairs we just arranged.

As Natalia undresses down to her bathing suit, my eyes linger across her sun-kissed skin. Her body is nothing short of mesmerizing. The suit hugs her figure beautifully, accentuating the curve of her hips and the enticing dip of her waist. The gentle swell of her breasts is undeniable, tempting my eyes to linger for just a moment longer.

She catches me looking, her eyes meeting mine, but she doesn't say anything. There's a hint of a knowing smirk on her lips, a silent acknowledgment of my attraction to her.

In her mind, I'm only here because we have a child to care for and a specific dynamic to navigate. So, I avert my gaze, letting my thoughts of being anything more with her go.

Despite Wendy's text message waiting for my response, my mind remains preoccupied with thoughts of Natalia. I'm well aware that she has made it clear she wants nothing beyond co-parenting with me, and I understand that our connection will never evolve into something more. Yet, the lingering thoughts and feelings persist, refusing to fade away.

Natalia settles herself onto the blanket, Remona in her arms, and I find myself watching them again. She peppers our daughter with kisses, each one soft and sweet. The sight melting the residual tension from our previous encounter.

Despite Natalia's distance with me, her love for Remi is boundless- it's a love that reaches beyond the stars.

I tend to notice the little things a lot- how tenderly she treats her. The way she gently cradles her. The way she holds our baby girl close as if to shield her from any harm that the world might bring. The soft lullabies she sings her to sleep.

And in response, Remi lights up every time her mother is near, her tiny hands always reaching out for her.

I love how Natalia playfully teases Remi, making silly faces and sounds just to earn a high-pitched squeal. She's patient with her, ever-ready to comfort her when she's fussy.

Maria shoves me out of my locked gaze on them. She leans over to Natalia, her eyebrow arched in question. "What's the dude's name again?" she asks, casting a sidelong glance in the direction Liam left.

Before Natalia can reply, Maria and I start throwing out guesses. "Lenny?" she suggests, a grin tugging at my lips.

I shake my head, "No, no, he looks more like a Larry."

"Or maybe a Lyle?"

"Lyle Lyle the crocodile." Maria mocks. "ooooh. Or could he be a Leo?" she chimes in again.

I snicker, "Or Lucas, the guy who probably thinks mustard is too spicy."

She smacks my shoulder, dying laughing, "Ooo, how about Lawrence? The name just screams, 'I collect stamps in my free time.'"

In the midst of our laughter, Natalia, clearly unamused, answers, "His name is Liam."

A shared 'oooo' echoes between Maria and I, as we nod vigorously.

"So, Liam is our vanilla flavor of the week then," Maria teases, enjoying the moment despite Natalia's annoyance.

She rolls her eyes at us, returning her attention to Remona, not allowing our banter to disrupt her quality time with our daughter.

My best friend seizes the opportunity to strike up another conversation. "Hey, Natalia, do you agree with LGBTQ rights?"

Nat nods, offering a simple "Mhmm" in response.

"But you aren't LGBTQ yourself. How would you define your stance?"

"Right... I'm just an ally."

With a mischievous glint in her eye, Maria quips, "An ally? An ally who aligned herself to this puta's dick."

Maria and I can't contain our laughter, finding the joke absolutely hilarious. However, Natalia doesn't share the same level of amusement. A fleeting smirk does manage to escape her lips as her gaze briefly meets mine, but she swiftly suppresses it.

She groans, standing up and grabbing Remona. "See, this is why I'm not hanging out with you two."

"No, wait, Nat, come back," I whine, reaching both my arms out to her.

She turns around, her expression slightly puzzled, unsure if I'm inviting her to sit with me or asking for a hug.

I clarify, my hands outstretched, "Give me my baby."

She rolls her eyes but ultimately hands Remona over to me. I kiss my daughter's head and smirk.

"Alright... You can go now."

As Natalia walks away annoyed, Maria bursts into laughter once again, exaggeratedly slapping my arm once more.

As the day unfolds, Maria and I bask in the warmth of the sun. We lounge on our beach chairs, soaking in the radiant heat while observing Natalia and Liam toss a frisbee back and forth.

My gaze often strays to her, particularly when her body moves with the catches of the plastic disc. The sight is hypnotic, her breasts bouncing with every successful catch.

Meanwhile, Bailey and Jeffrey had immersed themselves in their own world, frolicking along the shoreline. They seemed carefree and deeply in love.

After sleeping soundly for about an hour, seemingly unfazed by the surrounding beach noise, Remona is now sitting upright in her baby chair. Her large eyes wide and curious as she takes in the vibrant beach scene around her. She's contently gnawing on a toy, her tiny fingers exploring the object in her mouth with curiosity.

A familiar melody starts playing from the speaker on the blanket. It's the same song that was playing at the club when Natalia and I first met. The recognition is instantaneous, and I can see from Natalia's reaction that she's made the connection too.

"Oh shit, this is my jam!" Maria yells. She cranks up the volume before pulling me to my feet. The rhythm of the music guides us as we dance together, the beat syncing with our bodies as we move in a sensually charged rhythm.

I glance over and notice Bailey and Jeffrey dancing as well, their bodies entwined in their own beat. Natalia and Liam are also caught up in the music.

Seeing an opportunity, I reach for Bailey, switching partners. She gladly accepts, leaving Jeffrey with a giggle. I note Jeffrey not being the sensitive type and knowing his relationship with Bailey is secure, as he hypes her up in the dance with me.

Maria mirrors my actions, reaching for Natalia and pulling her away from Liam. Soon, all the girls are dancing while the men watch from the sidelines. Liam's smile is there, but it lacks Jeffrey's unashamed trust.

Maria then grabs Bailey from me and, with a smug smirk, gently nudges Natalia my way. Soon, it's her and I, our bodies moving together, our tempo sensual. The heat between us intensifies as we grind together to the beat of the music, laughter bubbling up between us.

Liam, however, doesn't share the same feelings. Jealousy flashes in his eyes as he forcefully pulls Natalia away from me, his grip on her arm clearly too tight.

"Ow, Liam! Let go," She yelps.

Without missing a beat, I pull his hand off her wrist. "What the fuck is wrong with you?"

Liam shoves me away. Balling my fist, I shoot him a glare but restrain myself, my eyes flicking to Remona, who's watching the scene unfold. "Do not cause a scene in front of my daughter."

His response is a dismissive laugh. "Your daughter? How's that even possible, bitch? You got a dick or something?"

"Care to check it out?" I counter, stepping forward, only for Natalia to block my path, her hand on my chest to stop me.

"Nah, two dykes can't make a baby. It's wrong," Liam sneers.

Natalia pauses, allowing his comment to sink in. She nods her head as if her mind is processing his words before swiftly spinning around, her fist connecting squarely with his jaw. She shakes her now limped hand, knuckles scraped and bloody from the impact, while he clutches his face in pain.

"Nothing about my family dynamic or my daughter is wrong, pinche pendejo," [fucking asshole] she fires back.

"You bitch," Liam seethes, only to be pushed away by the others.

"Get out of here, dumbass," Bailey barks at him.

"Fuck, that hurt," she frowns, still shaking her injured hand.

I inspect it gently, mindful of the fresh scrape on her knuckle. "Come with me," I say, then turn to the group. "Can you watch Remi?" The chorus of affirmative responses is instant.

I lead Natalia to a single-stall bathroom, shutting us inside and turning the lock. "Come here, let me see," I instruct, gently lifting her onto the counter. She complies gracefully, without questioning my guidance.

I grab some napkins, wet them, and carefully clean the blood and wound. "You did a number on his jaw," I comment, a hint of Pride in my voice.

"Yeah, well..." She winces slightly, her face scrunching up from the sting. "He said we were wrong," she voices, her tone uncertain.

All I can do is nod, staying silent as I let her air her thoughts.

"I mean, is it? You are a woman with a penis. I know it's different, but..." Her voice trails off.

"But?" I prompt, reaching for another paper towel to pat the cleaned cut dry.

"But... I don't think you're wrong. I think you're unique... and beautiful." she says, her words catching me off guard.

"Thank you," I manage to respond. It was at that moment that I became aware of our close proximity and the intimate positioning between us. I'm standing between her legs and at face level, close enough to take in her distinct scent, a subtle mix of orange blossom and the salty ocean air that clings to her skin from our day at the beach.

Natalia lowers her head. "Are we wrong? Having a daughter..."

"Stop," I cut her off before she can further question the worth of our existence, our family. I gently grasp her chin, tilting her face up to meet my gaze. "Nothing about this is wrong. Nothing about us having slept together is wrong. Nothing about the life we created is wrong. Please don't ever think that."

Our faces are now so close that our lips are barely an inch apart. I can feel her breath, warm and sweet, fanning against my skin. It takes all my strength to keep my eyes trained on her chin, avoiding her captivating gaze. But before I can retreat, her hand reaches up, pulling my neck down and crashing her lips onto mine.

It's like a taste of heaven, filled with an explosion of pent-up emotions and desires. It's urgent, yet gentle, a dance of lips and tongues, like two entities meeting for the first time yet already familiar with each other. My heart throbs in my chest, adrenaline pumping through my veins, and I can taste the sweet tang of her lip balm. Her hands find their way to my hair, tugging lightly as if she can't get enough.

She pulls away abruptly, out of breath. Pushing me from her, she scrambles off the bathroom sink and quickly crosses the small space to stand by the door. I'm left standing there, stunned and utterly confused by what just happened. I thought we were progressing, that we were moving towards something.

She pauses at the door, her hand on the knob. She sighs, rubbing her lips as if still savoring our kiss. "I am not g..." she begins but doesn't finish. She simply shakes her head and exits the bathroom, leaving me alone with my thoughts and the lingering taste of her on my lips.

CHAPTER 15

July 31, 2023

Dani

The dial tone plays in my ear, each rhythmic beat echoing in the silence of my truck. As I sit in the hospital parking lot, I hit redial for what feels like the hundredth time in the last three weeks. Once again, Natalia's voicemail greets me.

"Hey, it's Natalia. I can't take your call right now, but leave a message, and I'll get back to you as soon as I can. Thanks."

The chipper voice in the recording now feels like a cruel joke, its cheerful tone taunting me in this moment. Sighing, I disconnect the call, pocketing my phone as I step out of my truck.

The automatic doors slide open, and I step into the bustle of the hospital. The antiseptic scent wraps around me like an unwanted cloak. It's yet another day of numbness. Natalia has been silent for three whole weeks now, and each passing day makes me feel more isolated.

She hasn't answered my calls, my texts, or anything. It's as if a wall has suddenly sprung up between us. And the worst part of it all is I've been separated from Remona.

I try to busy myself with patient files, my fingers mechanically flipping through the pages. All the while, a hacky sack dances from hand to hand, the repeated motion a sad attempt to keep my mind off Natalia and my daughter.

A buzz from my phone snaps me out of my thoughts. My nerves flutter, hoping it's Natalia. But it's just Bailey again, sneaking me a lifeline with a picture of Remi. My chest clenches as I look at my daughter, her little face lighting up the screen. "You can come over after work."

I quickly type back, "Thanks, Bailey. See you tonight?"

The first week of this...silence...was tough but bearable. I thought maybe she needed space to process the kiss we shared. I didn't want to push her, so I let Remona stay with her the whole week. But as the days turned into weeks with no word from her, my worry morphed into frustration. This game she's playing, this deliberate avoidance... it's now becoming unbearable.

My calls go unanswered, my texts remain unread, and my heart continues to shatter piece by piece. I can't understand why she won't let me see Remona.

And it's not just Remona I miss. I miss her too. The way she smiles, the way she rolls her eyes at my lame jokes, her stubbornness. Despite the heated emotions between us, I miss her company, her voice.

Bailey has been a beacon of hope during all this. She's been sending me snippets of Remi's day, her way of letting me know that my daughter is okay. I cling to those updates; they're the only thing that brings an inch of peace.

The rest of the day passes in a blur of patients and paperwork. My usual work routine usually brings solace, but today it only amplifies my loneliness. Every cry of a newborn, every joyful laugh of a new parent, and every expectant mother reminds me of what I'm missing.

I start my night rounds, going from room to room, checking on the expectant mothers. I take their vitals, diligently noting the blood pressure, pulse rate, and oxygen levels and updating the patient charts accordingly.

"Good evening, Mrs. Thompson," I greet one of our regular patients, a warm smile on my face as I enter her room. "How did you sleep last night?"

Mrs. Thompson sighs, her hands rubbing her protruding belly. "Not so well, Dani. The baby kept me awake."

"I'm sorry to hear that," I sympathize, checking her vitals. "Why don't we try some gentle stretching exercises later tonight? It might help."

As the night progresses, I shift between different tasks - prepping rooms for incoming patients, ensuring the wards are stocked with the necessary supplies, updating patient records, coordinating with the doctors, and, most importantly, comforting the mothers-to-be.

During my dinner break, I sit in the break room, absentmindedly playing with my hacky sack. The mindless task is strangely soothing.

Around 7pm, I find myself conducting a prenatal class for first-time parents. I explain the stages of labor, breathing exercises, and pain management techniques, answering their countless questions.

The night draws to a close with a final round of patient check-ups. Just as my shift is about to end, Nurse Manager Johns hands me a folder. "She needs this surgery, Dani. Do your best."

I look down to see a photo of a worried-looking woman, pregnant and pale. The medical condition she has requires a cesarean section and subsequent surgery for her unborn child. While it's not immediately life-threatening, if left untreated, it could pose significant risks to both the mother and the baby.

I find the woman in her room, her eyes filled with fear and uncertainty. Her husband sits beside her, his face etched with worry. Their first child didn't survive a similar condition, and the trauma still lingers.

I approach them with empathy, knowing the delicate nature of the situation. I begin to explain the importance of the procedure, but the husband's focus seems solely on the well-being of the baby, disregarding the concerns for his wife.

"You're not touching my child. I won't let anything happen to him."

I take a deep breath, understanding the depth of his concerns but also recognizing the need to address the risks for both the baby and the mother. "I understand your worries, sir, but it's crucial to consider the potential complications for your wife as well. By proceeding with the surgery, we can increase the chances of a healthy outcome for both your child and your wife."

"I said you're not touching my child!" he snaps, his voice hard.

Annoyance floods me, but I swallow it down. "Your wife's life is at risk, too. This surgery could save both of them."

"I don't care about her," he spits back. "All I care about is my child!"

His words hit me like a slap. It's as if all the stress, all the misery of the past few weeks, explodes inside me. Suddenly, I'm not in a hospital room anymore—I'm back in my empty apartment, surrounded by the absence of Remona. I'm back in that moment, feeling the sting of Natalia's rejection.

"What the hell is wrong with you?" I explode. "She's your wife! She's carrying your fucking child! Her life matters, too!"

There's a shocked silence. The husband stands up, his face flushing with anger. "Who do you think you are telling me what to do?"

"Who am I? I am the one who's trying to save your wife's life, you ungrateful—"

"Dani!" A sharp voice cuts through the escalating argument. I turn to find Nurse Johns and Maria in the doorway, their faces pale with shock. Maria moves to stand between me and the husband, her hands raised in a calming gesture. "Dani, you need to step back," she says, her voice tight with concern. As we stand in the hallway, I can't contain my anger. "Hermana, your personal issues are affecting your work."

"This asshole doesn't give a shit about his wife!" I seethe, my voice rising despite myself.

Just as I finish my sentence, the door swings open, and Nurse Johns steps out, "Dani, that's enough!" Her eyes shoot daggers at me. "I don't know what's going on with you, but..."

"Seriously? He doesn't give a shit about her!"

"Stop!" Johns holds up a hand to silence me. "Their first child didn't make it, Dani. They are terrified; they are on edge. That's not an excuse for his behavior, but nor is it an excuse for yours. Your concern at that moment was to get her to sign the consent form for surgery, not argue with her husband."

I shake my head, my anger flaring again. "But--"

"No, Dani!" she interrupts me again, her voice firm. "You crossed a line. That woman might not trust our team now and might think the hospital can't control its staff's tempers to do the surgery properly. I have never seen you behave like this."

I open my mouth again, but she gives me a stern look. "Dani, your shift is over. Go home."

As Johns walks away, I'm left standing there, my hands shaking, a ball of anger welling up inside me. In a fit of rage, I punch a stack tray, sending papers flying everywhere. A woman nearby screams out in surprise and stumbles backward.

"What the hell!" she shouts.

I turn around, ready to snap back, but my words die in my throat as I recognize the woman I nearly hit. It's Wendy. She's staring at me wide-eyed, a mix of shock and fear on her face. My heart sinks.

"I'm sorry," I stutter out an apology, dropping to my knees to gather the scattered papers. To my surprise, Wendy drops down beside me, helping me collect the mess.

"Hey, no need to apologize to me," she says, her voice light and teasing. "Apologize to this tray of papers that got your wrath."

A surprised chuckle escapes me, easing the tension just a bit. "I'm sorry, papers," I say, playing along.

As we stand, she hands me what she picked up, her hand brushing against mine. "Anyone in particular that wrath is for?" she asks, a hint of curiosity in her eyes.

"No one in particular," I deflect, scratching the back of my head. I'm not ready to share my problems, especially with Wendy, whose text messages I've been avoiding for what seems to be no good reason. "Thank you for helping me clean up. I'll let you go."

Just as I'm about to walk away, she reaches out and gently grasps my wrist, halting my retreat. "Hey?" I pivot to face her, my eyes meeting hers. Her fingers idly trace patterns on my hand, an absent-minded gesture that manages to diffuse some of the tension coiling within me.

"Why haven't you answered my text?" she asks, her voice barely above a whisper, letting my arm go. "I thought everything between us was ...fine?"

"It is...I just..." I trail off, then grasp at a change of subject. "I'm sorry; what are you doing here at the hospital?"

"Oh, my sister's just down the hall, incubating baby number six," she replies, rolling her eyes for added effect. "I keep telling her the world has reached its quota for her line of mini-mes, but she's a bona fide baby factory. Pops them out like an overzealous vending machine."

"Mrs. Thompson?"

She nods, and we both laugh, the sound echoing in the almost empty halls. As our laughter dies down, she narrows her eyes at me. "Don't change the subject."

I find myself admiring her determination. She's relentless but kind. Something about her makes me want to open up, to let go of my problems for a while. After a moment, I pull out my phone and quickly type a text message, sending her a date and time - tomorrow at 7 PM.

She looks at her phone, her eyes lighting up with a smile. "I'm free," she says, her grin widening.

"See you tomorrow, Wendy."

She blushes, a pink tinge dusting her cheeks. "See you," she says softly.

Unable to help the faint grin that tugs at my lips, I nod and turn, making my way toward the locker room. I change quickly, swapping out my scrubs for my usual off-duty attire. I stride out of the hospital, climb into my truck and start the engine before pulling out of the parking lot.

I reach Bailey's house just past midnight, my mind racing with a thousand thoughts. I knock impatiently on her front door, bouncing on the balls of my feet. After what feels like an eternity, she finally opens the door.

"Hey." She offers me a soft, sympathetic smile, and I'm enveloped in a comforting hug.

"Hey." I accept the gesture, following her into the house.

Remona is sleeping soundly in her playpen. I'm immediately drawn to her, my heart aching at the sight of my sleeping daughter. "She's been asleep for a few hours," she comments softly, watching as I scoop Remona into my arms.

The infant stirs slightly, a scrunch on her face, but settles back to sleep once she's cradled against my chest. I sit on the couch, gazing down at her. She's grown so much in the five and a half months since she was born.

"When is she going to stop this? It's been three weeks." I whisper. "Thank you for letting me come over... again," I murmur, not taking my eyes off Remi.

"Of course," she responds without hesitation.

"Does she know I came over to see her?" I ask, my voice barely audible.

She hesitates for a moment before nodding. It's not surprising, considering she's Natalia's best friend.

"What even happened between you two?"

I run a hand through my hair, sighing. "We kissed."

"What!" she yells, startling Remona. I quickly shush her, rubbing Remi back to sleep.

I nod, my mind flashing back to the incident. "After she punched Liam... we were in the bathroom, and ... it just happened."

"Like you kissed her, or she kissed you?" she presses, her voice a whisper now.

"She kissed me."

"Wow," is all she manages to say.

"Right... Now she's dodging me like a bullet," I roll my eyes. "She won't answer my calls and is never home."

I glance her way, and she looks guilty. "Yeah, she's always here when you're off so that she won't run into you."

"That would have been good to know," I retort, annoyed at being kept in the dark.

She quickly interjects, "I'm not getting in the middle of this."

"You already are," I point out, gesturing to Remona and the room around us.

She sighs, "Right, that's just because I don't like the fact that she won't let you see Remona. You're still her mother regardless of what happens between you two. She's fighting against her beliefs, Dani."

I nod, fully aware of Natalia's internal struggle. "I know that already. But there is nothing I can do about it. I can't change her mind about me. And I'm tired of trying."

I grapple with my thoughts, understanding that if all Natalia seeks is co-parenting, I can swallow that bitter pill. Yet, the thought of being caught in a game of keep-away with my own daughter, pisses me off. I know I can't jeopardize my parental rights over a meaningless contest of who likes or dislikes me. Personal feelings take a back seat to Remona's well-being and our shared obligation as parents. "If co-parenting is all that she wants, then that's all she'll get from me for now on."

She nods in understanding. "I'll be sure to let her know."

I look around the room, my gaze searching for Jeffery. "He's out on the rig this week," Bailey answers my unasked question. Jeffery works in the oilfield and sometimes goes for a week or two at a stretch. "You can stay the night if you want."

She leaves the room for a moment before returning with a pillow and blanket. "Thank you," I murmur, my focus returning to the baby in my arms. I lay back on the couch, cradling Remona against my chest. I find myself kissing her forehead repeatedly, taking in her mother's familiar scent of orange blossoms that lingers in her hair.

Bailey's phone buzzes, and she gives me a small smile. "Goodnight, Dani." She quickly sends a text, her phone lighting up with an incoming call just moments later.

"Goodnight," I respond, my gaze following her as she moves away to take the call. She gives the person on the other end a quick "One second" before closing her bedroom door behind her.

A sigh escapes me as I settle back onto the couch. I'm aware she's most likely speaking to Natalia. However, I don't care about their conversation at this point. The only thing that matters to me is Remona. All I want is the ability to see my daughter without any restrictions. The idea of a court battle for visitation rights, or even custody, frustrates me.

CHAPTER 16

August 1, 2023

I spend the better part of my day with Remona, teaching her new sounds and words. It's the sweetest part of being a parent, watching her grow and learn. She's sitting up now, sturdy and determined, her big eyes taking in everything around her with such curiosity. Each day brings something new, and it's a privilege to witness her tiny triumphs.

We start our day with simple games. Games that are designed to stimulate her senses and motor skills. I give her a plush, brightly colored ball, one that's easy for her tiny hands to grip. I roll it toward her, and she watches it approach with an intense focus before clumsily reaching out to stop it. A smile blooms on her face each time she manages to grab it.

When we're not playing, I'm talking to her. Not in the high-pitched, cooing baby-talk voice that so many adults use, but in my regular, everyday voice. I narrate my actions, explain to her what I'm doing or about to do. I tell her stories, I sing songs, I ask her questions.

"See this, Remi?" I ask, holding up a square piece of brightly colored cloth. "This is a square. Can you say square?"

She stares at me, then at the square, her brow furrowed in concentration. "Squa..." she tries to mimic, not quite getting it right but trying nonetheless. I clap my hands, cheering her on, and she giggles, delighted at the attention.

I know she doesn't fully understand everything I'm saying. But that's not the point. Speaking to her like an adult, using regular vocabulary helps her language development. It exposes her to the richness of language, to the different sounds and rhythms, and intonations. It fosters a love for words and communication.

The game continues, a back-and-forth of sounds, expressions, and gestures, and I keep encouraging her to say 'mama.'

"Ma-ma," I repeat slowly, articulating each syllable so she can see the movements of my mouth. I place my finger on my lips to draw her attention there, watching as her gaze fixates on the motion.

"Ma..." she tries, the sound soft and tentative. A smirk of satisfaction flickers across her face as if she's pleased with her attempt.

"That's it, Remi," I praise, leaning closer. "Now try again. Ma-ma."

She seems to consider my instruction, her tiny brow furrowing in concentration. She mimics the movement of my lips, the first syllable coming out a bit more clearly this time. "Ma..."

"Now, the second part. Ma-ma," I encourage, my voice filled with anticipation. I can see her gears turning, and I can't help but hold my breath.

And then, suddenly, she screams it. "Mama!" Clear as day. As if she's been saying it her entire life.

A surge of excitement spreads through me. "Yes, that's right, Remi!" My voice rings out louder than I intended, echoing around the room. A chuckle rumbles up from deep within me, uncontainable. "That's me; I'm Mama!"

I pull her into a tight hug, peppering her face with kisses. She giggles, her small hands reaching up to pat my face. Our shared moments have a way of making the world fall away, time included.

Before I know it, the afternoon sun is beginning to dip lower in the sky. The shadows in the room shift, and I glance towards the clock. In the blink of an eye, it's already time for her next meal.

I carefully set her down on her play mat, surrounded by plush toys and bright rattles. As she busies herself with a toy giraffe, I make my way into the kitchen.

In the midst of my task of mashing bananas together, Bailey strides past, deeply immersed in a phone conversation. The familiar, slightly strained cadence of her voice tells me who it is before I even ask.

"If that's Natalia, tell her she should start introducing purees to Remi's diet," I say, glancing at her as she pauses her conversation to listen.

"The purees will not only provide her with necessary nutrients but will also help her get used to different textures and tastes," I continue, mashing the food in the baby bowl.

I stiffen at the sound of her voice on the other end. My hand instinctively tightens around the spoon's handle. Each press of my finger is a silent echo of the unanswered text messages from her. Each muffled word from the phone feels like a stab, a reminder of our broken communication. "She's asking about breastfeeding," Bailey says, relaying her question.

"Yes, she can continue breastfeeding." I wish I was having this conversation directly with her instead of relaying information through a middleman. But after last night's conversation with Bailey, I'm committed to respecting her space if that's what she wants. No more bombarding her with texts or showing up at her house unannounced anymore.

"But it's best to complement breastfeeding with the purees," I continue, "The combination of both will provide a balance of nutrients essential for Remi's growth and development."

Before Bailey can respond to me, the sound of her voice on the other end of the phone, distant and impersonal, twists a knot in my stomach again. I try to swallow the discomfort, focusing on the task at hand. "She said okay. Thank you," she relays the response, grabbing her laptop before retreating back to her room. I let out a sigh and shift my attention back to Remi, who is reaching out for her bowl.

Hours turn into a blur as I keep up with my daughter's boundless energy. I'm exhausted but content as I watch her play with her last burst of fuel, her eyes slowly starting to droop.

Just as the sun is dipping below the horizon, signaling the end of another day, Bailey reappears. She's been caught up in her work all day, tucked away in her room. "Natalia is on her way to pick up Remi," she informs me, and I nod, appreciating the heads-up.

"That's fine; I have somewhere to be tonight," I say, showering Remi's face with kisses before handing her over. Knowing Natalia's impending arrival, I pull Remi closer, cherishing the final moments of our day. A confrontation is the last thing I want right now.

I bid them goodbye and head back to my apartment. After a quick shower, I get dressed for my date with Wendy. I take a moment to look at myself in the mirror before leaving, pleased with what I see. I send Wendy a text, letting her know that I'm on my way, and then I'm off.

I head to a restaurant she picked out - a cozy little place down the street, its windows glowing invitingly. It's got a charm about it that's easy to appreciate. We meet, her warm smile immediately putting me at ease.

We settle into a corner booth, the background hum of conversation and occasional glass clink adding to the relaxed atmosphere. Our talk resumes from where we left it at the hospital yesterday. No awkwardness, just an easy back-and-forth that I appreciate.

As we dive into our meal, she has me laughing with a story about a recent disaster at her salon. "I swear, the lady strutted out with more confidence than ever with electric blue hair." She imitates the lady's walk, and I'm laughing so hard my sides hurt.

"I guess she felt like changing things up." She chuckles, her laughter infectious.

Thinking of hair-related fiascos, I remember my childhood. "Yeah, my mother used to come home with stories like that."

"That's right, she was a hairstylist too." I nod, and she smiles. "Do you still talk to her?"

Wendy's directness catches me off guard. I pause, a lump forming in my throat as I contemplate how to respond. I brush my thumb across the rim of my glass, a thoughtful frown tugging at my lips. It's a subject that carries a weight with it, one that often leaves me grappling for the right words. "Not as much as we used to," I admit, choosing my words carefully. "I remember the night I tried to explain to them about my intersexuality. The room had gone still, their faces a mix of confusion and disbelief as I voiced out loud what I'd felt inside for so long. I told them I was starting to identify with she/her pronouns, but their lack of understanding was mirrored back at me in their silence."

She takes in my words as a soft sigh escapes her lips. "I'm sorry, Dani," she says, her voice carrying a gentle sincerity. "No one should have to face that kind of misunderstanding, especially from their own family."

"It's okay. It happened a long time ago."

She takes this in, her gaze thoughtful. "So, growing up, you identified as a boy?"

A nostalgic smile touches my lips as I think back to my younger years. I shake my head. "Yes. I was society's typical boy growing up using 'he/him.' But things changed during puberty; I embraced being 'she' too."

My gaze drifts down to my outfit - a pair of comfortable, loose-fitting pants paired with a well-tailored button-up. It's simple but so very me.

"I've always leaned towards androgyny. I guess it reflects who I am on the inside."

I run a hand down my shirt, reflecting the duality I embrace. She chuckles, "I like your style; it suits you."

Our laughter and conversation carry us through dinner, and by the time we finish, the restaurant is beginning to empty out. She suggests a walk in the nearby city park, and I agree.

We head out of the restaurant and into the park next door. It's cooler now, the warmth of the day fading into a late evening. The conversation has been light and playful so far, but her story changes the mood. "It was tough," she says, her voice trembling slightly, "Steve and I just couldn't see eye-to-eye on anything anymore. The divorce was messy, and our fights over Tiffany... it was unbearable."

I can see the pain in her eyes. It feels all too familiar. I've been through my fair share with Natalia, battling for the right to see Remona. It's not the same, not a custody battle, but the fear of it escalating to that is always there.

"Wendy," I begin, my voice catching in my throat. I feel a knot in my stomach, but I know I need to be honest. "I've...I've really enjoyed tonight. You're incredible. But..."

"But because I am the mother of a child in your daughter's mother's dance class..."

"See, all the words just sound so complicated," I admit with a sheepish chuckle. She chuckles too, understanding my dilemma. "I don't want things to get messy. I'm dealing with some stuff right now... and I just don't think I'm ready for anything more than friendship at this point."

Her eyes sparkle under the park lights as she looks at me. "I appreciate your honesty. It's refreshing. And I'd be lying if I said I wasn't a little disappointed, but I get it. I really do."

"Thanks."

"Can we still hang out, though... as friends? Because after the divorce, I realized all my friends were actually Steve's friends... and I based my entire life off of my husband. And I really like hanging out with you. It just felt... easy."

She stops talking, and we're both grinning at each other. "Yeah. I'd like that." I steer us back toward the park, where we continue our walk. We delve back into a lighter conversation, the kind that doesn't require much thought but fills the space between us comfortably.

While I know there's not going to be anything more between Wendy and me, I can't help but appreciate her company. She's funny, kind, and understands what it's like raising a child in a less-than-ideal situation. And maybe, just maybe, that's exactly what I need right now.

chapter 17

September 15, 2023

Dani

It's a classic Friday night - the club is buzzing, and the air is thick with bass-heavy beats and bodies swaying in rhythm. I'm camped out at the bar, gripping a whiskey in my hand like a lifeline. The liquid fire dances down my throat, providing a much-needed buffer against the harsh reality.

Over on the dance floor, Wendy and Maria have claimed their territory. They are lost in their own world. Their bodies move as one with the music, their intoxication running deeper than the alcohol in their systems.

They're practically fused together on the floor, grinding and swaying to the rhythm. Every now and then, they steal kisses, not drunk and sloppy, but with a sweet tenderness that hints at something more. It's kind of fascinating watching their relationship unfold from the sidelines.

Over the past month and a half, they've become a constant in my life, something I really needed. Maria and my's duo expanded into a trio. I've watched them grow closer, my gaze catching their moments of shared laughter and lingering touches.

I'm happy for Wendy. It's good to see her find someone she can vibe with. And with Maria- I know she wouldn't hurt Wendy. It's honestly nice seeing my best friend finally let someone in.

I pretty much begged Maria to let Wendy tag along with us, and I'm glad I did. My friend turned into her friend, and now they're turning into something more. It's like I've been playing Cupid, and it feels good to see them so in sync.

But watching them, there's also a bittersweet twinge of nostalgia. It's hard not to remember the similar night I spent with Natalia. The dancing, the stolen kisses, the shared laughter, the connection. Those memories, bittersweet as they are, are all I've got right now. But for the moment, I'll just be here, cradling my whiskey and drowning in my thoughts.

***

September 16, 2023

The next morning, I wake up, squinting against the sunlight streaming through the half-drawn curtains of my bedroom. Groggily, I take in my surroundings, wondering how I ended up on the floor. I look towards my bed to find Wendy and Maria entwined in sleep, their faces peaceful and content. A small smile tugs at the corner of my lips. They look good together.

I close my eyes, hoping to get a few more seconds of shut-eye but hear a phone start ringing. It's quickly silenced as we all groan. Wendy is the first to finally get up, stepping over me carefully in nothing but Maria's long shirt and her panties. It's a sight I've grown used to over the past few weeks of sharing my space with them.

Weekends are our little adventures, the trio - Wendy, Maria, and me - always embarking on something new. Especially on the weekends when I don't have Remona. Life with Remona is like dancing on a tightrope, trying to find a balance between parenthood and everything else.

Natalia and I have carved out a set schedule for our daughter. I have Remona Monday through Thursday mornings, while Natalia teaches her dance classes. And then, she takes over in the evenings of the same days, when I go to the hospital. On weekends, from Friday to Sunday, we alternate who gets to have Remona. This schedule of ours, it's rigid, but it works.

Every morning, I make my way to the studio to pick up Remona. And every morning, I cross paths with Natalia. It's a brief moment, just a few seconds, but they're heavy with unspoken words. We always make eye contact, an intense gaze that's more a silent conversation than anything else.

But the only time we communicate or text is if one of us can't have Remona during our assigned times. Our conversations are always short, straight to the point, and strictly about our daughter. It's like we've drawn an invisible line, keeping our personal lives separate from our shared responsibility as parents. We've become experts at this game of silent exchanges and strict schedules, always dancing around each other.

Wendy walks off towards the bathroom, her movements slow and measured, a clear indication of her hangover. Meanwhile, I push myself off the couch, trailing behind Wendy toward the kitchen. The smell of brewing coffee fills the air, offering a sense of comfort and familiarity amidst the chaotic aftermath of our night out.

Leaning against the cool marble of the kitchen counter, I cradle my black coffee, the harshness combating the lingering taste of alcohol from the night before. Wendy appears at my side, a coy grin tugging at the corner of her mouth as she pours herself a mug. Her hair is in disarray, the look of the morning after painted all over her.

The silence between us is comfortable, familiar, as we stand side by side, sipping our coffee. I finally break the silence, my gaze flitting to the bedroom. "So, things are getting serious between you two, huh?"

She chuckles, staring down at her mug. "I really like her," she confesses, shrugging casually as she takes a gulp of her coffee.

I return her grin, nudging her with my shoulder gently. "I'm glad, Wen. You deserve someone good, someone like Maria."

"Yeah, and no offense to you, but I'm glad you passed me up but stayed my friend, because I would have never met Maria if it wasn't for that,"

I can't help but laugh at her statement, shaking my head. "None taken. I'm happy for you both."

Our quiet, coffee-fueled morning is abruptly shattered by Maria's distinct grumbling from the bedroom. "Headache!" she bellows out, and we instinctively flinch at her volume. "Wennnnn," she whines again, her voice strangely endearing despite the throbbing in my head. Wendy's chuckle beside me pulls my attention back to her.

"I better go in before she starts screaming for ibuprofen in that demanding voice of hers," She says, moving away from the counter.

I offer her a nod and a sympathetic smile, watching as she puts her coffee mug down and ventures into the lion's den - my bedroom. I've got no complaints about them occupying my room; their presence fills the silence in my condo on the days when Remi isn't around.

Seizing the moment of aloneness, I grab some clean clothes from my dryer and walk into the bathroom connected to Remi's room for a quick shower. The warm water is soothing, washing away the remnants of last night.

By the time I'm done and dressed, they emerge from my bedroom, giggles and inside jokes spilling from them.

"Hermana, you've got nothing here but baby food," she states loudly, rifling through my kitchen cupboards.

"Maria, please, your voice...." Wendy and I groan in unison.

Suddenly Maria's eyes light up. "Target run?" she proposes excitedly.

"No, babe, I'm tired," Wendy counters, sinking onto a stool at the counter, clearly ready for a nap.

Ignoring her protest, I chime in. "Target sounds good to me."

"Yes! Majority rules, baby," Maria declares, ignoring her girlfriend's feeble protests as she practically drags her towards the door to put on their shoes. I pick up my keys from the counter, trailing behind them.

As we step outside the building, the morning light hits us full force, causing us to wince and quickly don our sunglasses. The city is buzzing around us, oblivious to our hangovers, and I can't help but chuckle at the absurdity of it all.

At Target, we act like we're kids again, temporarily forgetting our adult responsibilities and headaches, indulging in silly antics.

Wendy and Maria take turns pushing each other in the shopping cart, bubbling with laughter as they speed down the aisles. They race each other, their elated squeals resonating around the store, earning us sidelong glances from the other shoppers.

We turn one aisle into a makeshift basketball court, throwing packets of chips into the shopping cart, whooping with victory each time we score.

We're laughing, we're a little loud, and we're definitely making a spectacle of ourselves. But it doesn't matter. For a little while, we're able to let go of everything else.

We're midway through an aisle when a familiar voice rings out, "Mamaaaa!" I freeze on the spot. Wendy, who has been standing on the front of the cart while Maria pushes it, doesn't stop in time and crashes into my back. The impact jerks me forward, making me almost stumble.

Seeing Natalia is always a punch in the gut, a swirl of emotions that never quite untangle. She's as stunning as ever, her grace effortlessly noticeable even in the humdrum of a Target store.

"Remonita!" I say instinctively. The moment I do, Natalia and Bailey turn around, their gazes landing on our trio. A series of emotions play across Natalia's face, one of them being surprise, I presume, at the sight of Wendy practically attached to my back. I'm aware of the position we're in, one that could easily be misconstrued, so I gently move out from her grip, trying to avoid any awkwardness.

Wendy and Maria, both chuckle, sensing the undercurrent of tension. Maria, acting on a whim or maybe just to break the tension, grabs Wendy's hand and pulls her into a soft kiss. Their momentary distraction successfully softens Natalia's expression for a second, and I am grateful for their light-hearted antics. Maria, grinning like a Cheshire cat, manages to gently coax Wendy away from me, and they disappear down another aisle.

With them conveniently disappearing, I'm left facing Natalia and Bailey. However, my gaze is drawn toward the cart carrying my little conejita. She stretches her tiny arms toward me, her babbling voice beckoning. I step forward, my heart fluttering as I pull her into my arms and plant a soft kiss on her chubby cheek.

"What are you doing here, little one?" She jabbers in response, her little hands reaching for my hair.

Natalia's voice pulls me out of my trance, "We're picking out some clothes for her. She's outgrown most of the ones she has now." she says sheepishly.

I look down at Remi, now seven months old, growing so quickly that she's too big for her clothes. Thanks to my genes, she's larger than average. I'd noticed her growth spurt last week and bought some clothes for her, intending to send them over to Natalia's place for the weekend.

"I noticed," I reply, "I got her some clothes too, for my house. I'll send some over with her this weekend."

She tries to cut in, a hint of her old stubbornness surfacing, "Dani, you don't have to..."

But I quickly dismiss her protest, "No, it's..."

"We found it!" Maria yells, holding up a pill bottle triumphantly as if it's a priceless artifact. Wendy, on the other hand, is laughing, an armful of snacks balancing precariously in her arms.

"I should probably go," I manage to say as Maria and Wendy make their way over to us, their faces beaming.

My eyes catch sight of Remona's favorite snacks on a nearby shelf. I grab a packet and toss it into Bailey and Natalia's cart. "They're her favorite," I explain, and Natalia thanks me, her voice barely above a whisper.

"Bye, baby," I lean over to give Remi a parting kiss on her cheek. The way she's positioned in Natalia's arms, my face comes dangerously close to hers. I feel her breath hitch, and for a moment, we're caught in a silent exchange, our eyes locked on each other. It feels like we're the only two people in the store until Bailey gently pulls Natalia away, breaking the moment.

Maria and Wendy, on the other hand, are tugging me in the opposite direction. As I take one last glance at Natalia and Remona, I'm swept away by my friends, their laughter echoing in the store.

CHAPTER 18

September 16, 2023

Natalia

The moment Dani and I lock eyes, my breath hitches. It's always like this - seeing her sends a surge of emotions through me. The way she smiles at Remona, the tender care she displays. There was a time when those smiles were for me, and the memories of it crashes over me in waves.

Every morning, as I teach my dance class, I catch glimpses of her in my peripheral vision, coming to pick up Remona. Our eyes meet sometimes, but there are no words exchanged. An invisible wall separates us, built from our shared pain and disappointment.

Our arrangement with Remona is strictly scheduled and adhered to. As much as this agreement is in the best interest of our daughter, it also distances me from Dani, maintaining a much-needed barrier.

It wasn't that I intended to keep her away from Remi. In those three weeks following our kiss in the bathroom, I was too scared to be around her, too afraid to be alone with her. I feared that our unresolved feelings would rise to the surface, that I wouldn't be able to hold back the tangle of emotions I felt for her.

There were times when I would watch her from the security cameras at the dance studio. She would arrive at the studio and park in the parking lot, waiting patiently for us. Some days, she'd even use her key to get inside, waiting for us there. Every single time, I'd watch from the safety of Bailey's house, waiting for her to leave before I returned home.

I knew what my heart wanted - to run to her, apologize for that day in the bathroom, for keeping Remona from her. I wanted to tell her that it wasn't intentional, that I was scared of the feelings I held for her. But every time, my mind and beliefs held me back, telling me it was wrong to harbor such feelings, that I shouldn't entertain them. This internal battle wore me out, and I hated it.

Caught in my musings, I hardly notice Bailey pulling me towards the Starbucks in the store, our shopping trip momentarily forgotten.

"What was that?" She questions me as soon as we find seats in the Starbucks corner, her stern tone immediately putting me on the defensive.

"What was what?" I respond, feigning ignorance about the close moment that had transpired between Dani and me minutes ago.

"Natalia, you cannot keep playing this game with her," she reprimands me, her gaze piercing.

"I'm not playing anything. She was just saying bye to Remi."

"Yeah, and damn near almost kissed you again." I roll my eyes at her. I didn't even tell Bailey about the kiss; Dani did. I would have taken that secret to my grave, but now I hear about it from my best friend like clockwork.

"You need to figure your shit out," she scolds before striding off to get our coffees.

As I watch her walk away, I pull Remona onto my lap. "Mamaaa," she coos, pointing towards the entrance of the store where Dani, Maria, and Wendy are exiting. Dani's eyes remain fixed on us until she disappears from view.

"When did Wendy and Maria get together?" I ponder aloud, more to myself than anyone else.

"I don't know, maybe around the time you and Dani were locking lips in the beach bathroom," Bailey quips, appearing again with two drinks in her hands. I glance around nervously at her loud words.

"Aww, come on, Natty. No one gives a shit about being a lesbian. It's 2023, damnit." A group of teenagers nearby chuckles, and I roll my eyes.

"Could you say it louder for the whole world to hear?"

"Oh, you want me to say it loud enough for your God too?" I sigh with frustration, standing up and walking away, Remona perched on my hip.

The car ride back to the studio is silent. We unload the groceries, and I notice Bailey's huffing and puffing as she passes by me.

"What is the matter with you?"

"Nothing. The two of you are getting on my nerves. This back-and-forth shit."

"There's nothing back and forth happening."

"Yeah, okay. Because I'm just delusional."

"Yeah. That. Exactly."

She starts, "You need to face the facts."

"And what might those be?" I challenge her.

"You slept with a woman who has a penis. She gave you a daughter. You found her again. She has shown you she is very much interested in you and wants to raise your daughter together. And you are also very, very, very, very...."

"Okay, okay, I get it."

"But do you though, Nat? Because if you got it, you would accept it."

"It's not that easy."

"But it is. It is that easy. Give in to your feelings. Stop playing with hers."

"I'm not playing with her feelings."

"Lie."

"And I don't have feelings."

"Lie again."

"Bae, I'm not."

"Thou shall not lie. Ninth commandment - Thou shalt not bear false witness against thy neighbor," she says, her eyes full of challenge this time.

"No. Don't"

"Matthew 7:1-2 - Do not judge, or you too will be..." she continues, her voice becoming a hammer pounding against my walls.

"Bae."

"Second Commandment - love thy neighbor...Matthew 22:36-40 - Love is the greatest commandment."

"Bailey, stop," I plead, a knot forming in my stomach.

"John 13:34-35 - Love one another... John 4:7-8 - Love comes from God," her voice is steady, relentless.

With each verse she recites, my defenses crumble a little more, my eyes begin to water.

"1 Corinthians 13:4-8 - Love never fails... 1 John 4:18 - There is no fear in love,"

"Please... Please... stop," I plead, my voice a mere whisper now.

"Romans 8:38 - Nothing can separate us from the love of God...."

"Stop!" I manage to cry out. I try to hold back my tears and catch my breath, but Remi is startled by my outburst and starts crying. I quickly pick her up, finding comfort in her as much as she finds in me. "Get out," I say calmly.

"Nat..."

"I said get out!" She sighs before grabbing her purse and walking out the door. And I am left alone with my daughter and my own conflicting emotions.

Soothing Remona back down for her evening nap took a few more minutes than usual. Bailey's words were still echoing in my mind. Once Remi's soft breathing signals that she asleep, I carefully lay her in her crib, which I'd recently moved back into my room.

The familiar sight of her sleeping peacefully does little to calm the storm brewing within me. I pause for a moment, taking a few deep breaths to regain my composure before heading back to the kitchen.

As I unload the rest of the groceries, I come across the bag of Remi's favorite snacks that Dani slipped into our cart. The thought that she knows these little details about our daughter's likes and dislikes has my fingers trembling as they trace over the bag, and something about it brings a fresh wave of tears.

Desperate for a lifeline, I grab up my phone, scrolling through my contacts until I find the number that I've so long avoided. It's filled with serious text messages now, all related to Remi's schedule and nothing more. Before I could second-guess my actions, I hit the call button.

The phone rings, each tone sending a pulse of anxiety through my chest. It feels like an eternity before the call connects, and I'm on the brink of hanging up when I hear a voice on the other end.

"Hello?" Her voice is — smooth and soothing, even across a phone.

It tugs at something deep inside me, and I'm crying again. "Nat?"

"Yea..." I manage to whisper.

"What's wrong?" she asks, genuine worry threading through her words.

"I..." I hear the echo of laughter and the murmur of conversation on the other end of the line. The reminder that she's with Maria and Wendy gives me a moment of clarity.

"Nat?" she prompts again when I don't answer. "Is Remona okay? Do you need me to come over?"

"She's okay. And n...no. I'm okay. Sorry, I called," I reply, the words coming out in a rush before I quickly disconnect the call. I stare at my phone for a moment, cursing myself for calling in the first place.

With a sigh, I wipe my tears and put away the last of the groceries. I prepare Remona a nighttime bottle, and after ensuring she's settled and feeding properly, I head to the shower with the baby monitor.

Once I'm clean and changed into a big shirt and panties, I close the door behind me, wanting to ensure Remona gets a peaceful night of rest.

I find myself gravitating towards the couch with a large bowl of popcorn, a box of tissues, and the TV blaring at a volume that would usually be considered inappropriate. Thankfully, with no immediate neighbors and my daughter's deep, storm-proof slumber, I have the solitude I need in this moment.

For some unknown reason, when I'm in a miserable mood, I tend to seek out movies that only promise to worsen it. So, here I am, losing myself in the emotional turmoil of Loving Annabelle, my tears flowing freely as the movie unfolds.

Three-fourths through the film, I hear keys jingling at my door. My body tenses, my pulse quickening as the door creaks open, revealing a familiar silhouette, visible only in the dim light filtering through the blinds. I turn the tv volume down.

"What are you doing here?" I ask, hastily wiping my tears away.

"You were crying," Dani says simply, carrying a gentle concern. She places her keys down and kicks her shoes off.

"I said you didn't need to come over."

She takes a few steps closer, her brow furrowing in worry. "Is Remi okay?"

"She's fine," I reply, my voice wavering despite my best efforts to keep it steady.

"Then why were you crying?"

"I said I was fine, Dani." My tone is sharp, a sudden flash of frustration consuming me.

But she, unswayed, stands her ground. "You aren't."

"I am."

With a sigh that echoes loudly in the quiet room, she starts to put on her shoes. "Okay, then I'll go."

"Wait, no." My words sound desperate, even to my own ears.

She groans, halting in her tracks, as her keys clink against each other. "Why? All you do is push me away."

"I'm sorry." I say staring at the bowl of popcorn in my lap.

"Sorry isn't going to cut it. This roller coaster with you is tiring."

"You don't think I'm tired of it too?"

"I'm not sure what you think. You never let me stay around long enough to figure it out." I remain quiet, unable to contradict her. "You're in denial."

"No, I'm not." I furrow my brows.

"You are," she insists.

"Denial about what?" I laugh a humorless chuckle, attempting to brush off her accusation.

"That you like me,"

"No," I begin to shake my head.

"That you feel something for me," she pushes.

"No,"

"That you liked the kiss,"

"No," my head still shaking in a constant loop. "No," I whisper again, faltering under her steady gaze.

"Okay then, I'm leaving. I have somewhere to be." She pivots towards the door, and a jolt of panic seizes over me. In an instant, everything in my lap scatters onto the floor.

"Wait, no," I blurt out, stumbling towards her.

"No, what, Natalia?"

"Just...no, okay?" I insist, hands running agitatedly through my hair. My mind caught in a maelstrom of clashing emotions as I scramble to put my words in order.

"No, you don't want me to stay?" she seeks clarification, her stare intense. But even I don't know what I mean, I just keep saying it.

"No," I repeat, instantly regretting it. I meant to say yes. Yes, stay. Why is my brain doing this?

"Okay." She reaches for the doorknob.

"Wait, no... yes. Yes, please stay," I plead, my voice desperate, my heart pounding in my chest.

"For what?" Her tone is calm, as if she's trying to decipher a riddle. "For what?" My throat tightens as more tears threaten to spill. "Natalia, what do you want?"

"I don't know, okay!" I explode, holding back the tears that threaten to spill.

"If you can't figure it out, how am I supposed to? You're so confusing. I shouldn't have even come." Before she can open the door, I move in front of her, blocking her path.

"Please..."

"What do you want?!" She demands, her patience evidently running thin. I'm crumbling under the weight of my emotions, my heart fells like it's going to shatter into a million pieces. "Natalia, what do you want!!"

"I want you!" I finally confess, my voice cracking from the strain of my own desperation. "I wa..." The tears are free now, streaming down my face, carrying with them the anguish of my denial. "I want you. I want all of this...whatever 'this' is. I want us to raise Remi together, to share every moment of joy, every milestone, every setback."

She looks at me, evaluating the sincerity in my words. "So this is just about Remona again?"

"No! God, no! It's not about Remona. It's not just about our daughter," My voice is trembling, my hands are shaking. I inhale deeply as if the air has suddenly turned thin, filling my lungs with vulnerability. "I like you, Dani. God, I like you so much that it terrifies me. Every time you're around me, it feels like I'm fighting a losing battle just to keep breathing. And when you leave... when you leave, it's like you've stolen all the air that gives me the strength to live."

My words come out in a rush as I move past her, pacing across the room. The hard wooden floor beneath my feet does little to ground me; it feels like I'm floating in a sea of uncertainty.

"I crave your presence with every breath I take. Every smile, every touch, every lingering glance... it sets my soul on fire." Our shared memories flicker through my mind, feeding the flames that burn within me.

I stop mid-pace, finally meeting her gaze. "But denying it... denying these feelings... it's suffocating me," I admit, choking on my words. "The weight of this denial has become unbearable, constricting my every breath, and I want to break free.... I need to." I suck in ragged breaths. "I ne.. I need to be with you Dani." my heart pounds fiercely against my ribcage, as my tears continue to spill from my eyes.

The silence between us stretches on, my words hanging heavy in the air. And then, without uttering a single word, she bridges the gap between us. Her hand lifts, tenderly brushing away my tears with a softness that's almost heartbreaking. And before I can fully register what's happening, she's pulling me in, sealing my confession with her lips on mine.

CHaPTer 19

S eptember 16, 2023

Natalia

Her lips on mine send me off balance, igniting a flood of emotions. The kiss is tender and soft, like a whisper against the commotion inside me.

Her tongue slides over mine in a slow, deliberate movement that steals my breath away. The taste of her is more intense than anything I've ever experienced. It's as if every nerve ending in my body has awakened, responding solely to her.

My fingers find their way to her hair, tangling in the strands as I pull her closer. The beat of my heart echoes in my ears, drowning out everything else.

Without thinking, I lead her backward. My hands glide down her arms, finally settling on her waist. She backs into the front door, a hard thud reverberating in the quiet house. Her lips part from mine, tracing a path down my jawline. Each kiss ignites a spark on my skin, goosebumps following in the wake of her touch as I surrender to her.

I become acutely aware of her groin against my thigh. This intimate pressure sends a jolt of heat through me, reminding me of our close proximity. Even through our clothes, her warmth is a tempting hint of what might transpire between us. "Shit," the word slips from my lips in an effort to steady the chaos brewing within me.

She ceases her movement, pulling back to gaze at me, her chest heaving from the shared exertion. "Do you want me to stop?" She asks, her eyes reflecting a hint of concern. I take a deep breath, my words lodged somewhere in my throat, leaving me unable to respond.

"Do you want me to leave?" Her question cuts through the electric tension, shattering the intoxicating bubble we were enclosed in.

My mind battles internally, religious beliefs and societal voices condemning my feelings. This part of me screams to push her away, reclaim the safety of obedience, and cloak myself again in the comfort of a well-trodden path.

Yet, my heart is the part of me that pulses with its own rhythm. It's a melody of desire, an unsuppressed longing for her. This part of my being cherishes the warmth of her touch, the softness of her lips, the connection I've found in her arms. It urges me to ignore the doctrines, to cast off guilt and shame, and to embrace my own truth.

I'm torn, caught between the two. But when I look into her eyes, they are filled with patience and understanding. It's enough for my heart's voice to grow louder, drowning the condemning whispers of my mind.

With my swollen lip caught between my teeth, I shake my head 'no.'

"Can you... just stay with us for the night?" I manage to ask, the words barely audible.

She leans in to capture my lips in another searing kiss before pulling away. "Come," the single word wraps around me like a soothing blanket, beckoning me to follow her. It's a temptation I cannot resist. I allow her to guide me to my bedroom, where Remona lies peacefully asleep in her crib.

She lifts off her shirt, cool air tracing her defined abs. I can't help but stare at her sculpted body, my gaze lingering on the swell of her breasts cupped in her sports bra. The view causes a twinge of desire to flare within me, igniting my skin where her touch has been.

She approaches the bed, the moonlight casting her figure in an ethereal glow. As she crawls on the mattress, she turns to me, her eyes inviting, not pushing. She's giving me the choice, the power to decide what I want. My decision doesn't take long, drawn by the heat radiating from her.

She slips into the bed, her body molding against mine as she pulls the blanket over us. The scent of her is intoxicating, a mix of sandalwood and citrus. It's a scent I want to memorize, even in my dreams. I close my eyes, allowing myself to surrender to the calmness her proximity brings.

But just as I'm sinking into this peaceful abyss, reality crashes over me. The tears come uninvited once more. Each one is a silent testimony to the fears I've been holding back. I feel her stiffen, then gently turn me around to face her.

Her eyes soften. "Nat, baby, nothing about this is wrong. Please just let me in," she pleads. Her hand tenderly wipes my tears away before pulling me back into her arms. Her lips find my forehead, planting soft, reassuring kisses until I feel my uncertainties ease once more.

Exhaustion eventually wins over my internal struggles. Wrapped in her strong arms, her heartbeat lulls me to sleep, helping me find peace in her embrace.

***

September 17, 2023

My eyes slowly flutter open, my hand reaching out to feel the cool, vacant space beside me. For a moment, I think the previous night was all a figment of my imagination, a dream too beautiful to be real. But then, soft giggles float in from the other room, a captivating sound far too real to be part of any dream.

Rubbing my eyes, I swing my legs over the side of the bed, tugging on my loose shirt as I get up and venture toward the source of the noise. Peeking around the doorway, my heart melts at the sight before me.

Dani, glowing in the morning light, is holding Remona's tiny hands, guiding her in a little dance to the beat of bachata. Their laughter fills the room, a sound that makes me smile.

My gaze lowers to the wooden floorboards, the memory of last night rushing back. The kissing, the comforting embrace, the tears... I touch my lips, still able to feel the lingering sensation of her lips on mine, the memory causing my heart to flutter.

A sudden movement catches my attention, drawing me back to reality—Remi standing proudly on her own little feet. A wide smile instantly graces my face as I stride over to her, unable to contain my joy. "Good morning, mijita," I coo, sweeping her into my arms. I look around, scanning the room and realizing Dani is no longer there. Drawn by the smell of cooking, I wander into the kitchen.

I nestle my body against her back, leaving gentle kisses along her shoulders. She turns off the stove, placing the last golden pancake on a stack before turning around to relieve me of our daughter.

Remona, now on the floor, quickly gets distracted by a nearby toy. As my attention shifts to the ground, She reaches up, gently cupping my chin, drawing my gaze back to her.

"Are you okay?" she asks, her eyes filled with genuine concern. I shake my head 'no,' not trusting myself to speak. But I lean in, pressing my lips to hers before breaking away and resting my head against her chest. Her arms circle me, holding me close.

"I need to go somewhere after breakfast," I mumble against her.

Without pulling away, she gives a nod. "I'll stay and watch Remona," she offers, her willingness bringing a soft 'thank you' to my lips.

Breakfast is almost too normal for the commotion twirling inside my head. We share stolen glances, laughter, casual touches, each a glimpse of the life I find myself drawn to, and yet, not sure if I'm allowed to desire.

With the dishes washed and put away and my attire meticulously chosen, I find myself frozen in place, my gaze fixated on the clock. Dani and Remi are seated on the floor, engrossed in a playful display of colorful building blocks. "I don't..." I begin to say something wanting to talk myself out of what I'm about to do.

"Go. It's okay. We'll be here when you get back."

I sigh before nodding. I bend down, pressing a soft kiss to Remona's chubby cheek; her giggles echo in my ears, a sound that would be my anchor in the moments to come.

Stepping out of the studio, the comforting hum of my house is quickly replaced by the exhilarating embrace of the cool morning air.

My mind is occupied with spinning thoughts as I maneuver the curving roads. Time slips away like sand through my fingertips until, almost by instinct, I find myself standing on the steps of the church where I spent my youth.

The sun's rays dance across the stained glass windows, splattering the front with brilliant hues. Nostalgia mixes with fear as I consider the weight of what I'm about to do.

This is the church my parents and I attended religiously. I'd never imagined I'd be back here after they died, standing on the threshold of a past I thought I'd left behind. Yet, here I am, half-convinced that I might burst into flames the moment I step inside because I have feelings for a woman. Ridiculous, I know, but fear has a knack for painting the absurd as reality.

I climb one step, then two, my heart pounding with every bit of uncertainty. Halfway up, I turn around, debating whether or not I should just go back down. I stand there, trapped in hesitation, before I eventually brace myself and return to the church's entrance.

Taking a deep breath, I push the heavy wooden doors open and step into the quiet interior. The smell of incense and old paper floods my senses, stirring memories I thought were long forgotten. Despite my fears, there's a strange comfort in the familiarity.

I gravitate towards the holy water font, dipping my fingers in the water as I've done countless times before. Crossing myself, I kiss my fingers — an old habit that surprisingly hasn't lost its touch.

The confession booth waits ominously, a wooden box that's about to become the holder of my secret. Slipping inside, I sit in the confined darkness, waiting for the priest to initiate the ritual. My heart feels like a wild animal in my chest, pounding with anticipation and anxiety.

"Forgive me, Father, for I have sinned," I speak, my voice echoing slightly in the small space. "It's been four years since my last confession."

The voice on the other side is kind, patient. "Welcome back, my child. May the grace of God be with you. What burdens your heart today?"

I suck in a breath, clinging to the shreds of my courage. "Father, I... I think I'm falling for a woman."

The silence stretches on, its weight so heavy, so palpable, as though I can reach out and touch it. It presses down on me, filling me with a growing dread that makes my heart pound against my chest.

In my mind, I can almost see the gates of hell opening up beneath me, ready to swallow me whole. The vivid imagery of fire and brimstone, born out of years of religious teachings, manifests itself in my mind's eye. The fear is so real, so tangible, I can almost feel the searing heat licking at my feet.

And just as I'm about to succumb to this dreadful anticipation, the priest's voice breaks through, dispelling the haunting images, "My child, love is a divine gift. It knows no gender. It knows no bound-aries. It is not our place to judge but to accept and cherish all forms of love. Love, in all its expressions, can lead us closer to Him, as long as it's pure, genuine, and respectful."

His words reverberate through the small space of the confessional. It feels like a plunge into icy water, the shock stripping away all previous thoughts, making the world outside this tiny box ceases to exist.

My eyes blink rapidly as I try to comprehend his words. "But... isn't it a sin?" I stammer; the words taste bitter on my tongue. "Won't I... won't I be punished for having these feelings for her?"

His voice filters through the mesh, calm yet firm, "Sin arises from actions that cause harm, from selfishness and cruelty. What you're describing is love. It's caring for another person, wanting to protect them and make them happy. There is no sin in love."

"Love..." I murmur the word like it's foreign, unfamiliar. It's a terrifying thought - that these deep, swirling emotions I have for Dani might be love. For so long, I've done everything I could to keep them at bay. I dated men, distanced myself, convinced myself that we were tied only by Remona. But no matter how hard I tried, my feelings for her would always surface.

"But what if I'm not ready to call it love? What if I want to take it slow, figure things out?"

"There's nothing wrong with that. Love isn't a destination; it's a journey. It's about exploring and understanding your feelings at your own pace. As long as your actions come from a place of respect and care, you're on the right path."

"But the teachings...the Bible..." I trail off, my mind spinning. Everything I've been told, everything I've been taught, it's all crashing down around me, crumbling into dust.

"The Bible teaches us to love one another," the priest continues, his calm voice cutting through my turmoil. "It's a guide, not a rulebook. It's up to us to interpret it in a way that brings us closer to God and to each other. And if your love for this woman does that, brings you closer to the essence of kindness, generosity, and love that God embodies, then I see no sin in it."

The priest's words seep into my being. My eyes well up with tears as a surge of relief floods over me. For the first time in a long time, I feel seen, understood, accepted.

"I'll leave you to your thoughts, my child," I hear his departure, leaving me in a pool of solitude to reflect on his words.

After a few silent moments, I gather myself, stepping out of the confession box and into the vast expanse of the church. A few people kneel at their pews, heads bowed in silent prayer. I walk past them, making my way to the votive stand.

A large array of unlit candles stand before me, waiting to be lit. Picking up a taper, I ignite it from an already burning candle and proceed to light two candles—one for Mami and one for Papa. The tiny flames flicker and dance in the semi-darkness.

"Hi, Mami... Hi, Papa..." I murmur, "I've... I've finally made it back to the church," I continue, a soft sigh leaving my lips. "I'm not as scared in this world without you two anymore."

I pause, gathering my thoughts before voicing my deepest worry. "Please, if you can... give me a sign. Show me that the path I'm on is okay, that you support me in this... in everything."

Letting out a sigh of resignation, I half-expect silence in response, the absence of a sign reflecting their disapproval. But suddenly, a gust of wind sweeps through the church as someone exits through a door nearby. Instinctively, I brace myself, fully expecting the tiny flames to be extinguished. But to my surprise, the wind does not blow out the candles.

Instead, it gently fans the flames, causing them to leap up and touch the unlit wicks of the surrounding votive candles. In a matter of seconds, the entire stand is a sea of twinkling lights, casting a warm, gentle glow around me.

For a moment, I stand there, stunned, my hand covering my mouth. Then, an uncontrollable giggle escapes my lips. I wipe my tears away and smile. "Thank you, Mami, Papa," I whisper, a warmth spreading in my chest. With a final look at the sea of lights, I turn around and head towards the exit, my heart a little lighter than before.

When I reach the house, the door closes behind me with a soft click, sealing off the outside world. Kicking off my shoes, I place my purse on the side table, reveling in the quietness of my home.

A quick scan around reveals no sign of Dani or Remona. Their absence nudges me toward our bedroom, my heart swelling at the sight that greets me. Dani is sprawled out on the bed, one arm laid protectively around our little girl. Remi is curled up next to her, milk drunk from a bottle of my pumped breast milk, a tiny dribble still lingering on her rosy lips. I release a soft chuckle, realizing I'm the reason behind most of Remi's co-sleeping nights.

Unable to resist the pull of the intimate scene, I tiptoe over and crawl into bed, curling up behind Dani. My frame is a little smaller than hers. I press my face into the exposed skin of her shoulder blades, her sports bra leaving a good amount of skin bare for me to nuzzle. I breathe in her scent, familiar and comforting, and place a soft kiss on her warm skin.

She stirs awake at the contact, a soft groan escaping her lips. Gently, she rolls onto her back, carefully maneuvering our baby so she lies on her chest. Remi's eyes flutter open, a wide grin breaking out on her face at the sight of me, revealing a hint of her first tooth peeking through her gums. I run my fingers over her cheek, the soft motion lulling her back into sleep.

"Where'd you go?" Dani's voice is husky with sleep, her words slightly slurred.

"To the church," I reply, my eyes never leaving our daughter. I feel her fingers on my cheek, mirroring the motion of mine. "I'm okay," I whisper, preempting the worry that I know is lingering in her touch.

Slowly, I raise my head, seeking her lips with mine. My tongue tracing the contours of her mouth, discovering uncharted territory that sends thrilling shivers down my spine.

Her taste is enticing, like a sweet elixir that keeps luring me back. Though I've kissed her before, this time it's profoundly different. This moment, I am entirely present, fully allowing myself to experience the depth of my feelings for her.

Our daughter begins to stir between us with a soft whimper, forcing us to break our connection. Her hand instinctively soothes Remi with a tender rub on her back, quickly settling her.

I nestle my head against her chest, comforted by her nearness. "Thank you for being patient with me," I whisper.

"Of course," she replies before pressing her lips to my temple. She settles back into the pillows, her breathing evening out as she follows Remona into the land of dreams.

As I watch them both, my heart swells. I'm home, surrounded by them, and for the first time in a long time, I feel truly at peace.

***

The End

Milton Keynes UK
Ingram Content Group UK Ltd.
UKHW020803241123
433194UK00016B/991